SPRING AT THE STABLES ON MUDDYPUDDLE LANE

Heart-warming, uplifting romance

Etti Summers

For my Dad... for taking me riding all those times, when he would have preferred to be doing something – **anything** – else x

CHAPTER ONE

Early morning was the best time of day, as far as Petra Kelly was concerned. And by early morning, she really did mean early, because when you had animals to see to you couldn't spend half the day lazing around in bed, no matter how comfy and warm you felt. By six a.m. she'd already freed an excited cluck of chickens from their overnight prison (in other words, the coop), had fed them, and had collected the warm brown eggs from the straw. She left the chickens to squabble and squawk over the grain she'd spread on the ground, and went off to check on Princess.

She always saw to the chickens and the goat first because they were the creatures which caused her the greatest headache if she left them until later. The chickens would make a racket and refuse to lay, and the goat kicked the walls of her stall and bleated incessantly.

Princess was on her hind legs with her front ones on the half-open door of her stall as usual Petra noticed, as she entered the barn. Petra had built a goat-proof stall for her on one side of the building, so the animal could see out but couldn't get out. Which was a good thing, because if she was left to her own devices, she'd eat everything she could get her sharp little hooves on.

The goat bleated loudly as Petra opened the barn door, Queenie hot on her heels. The dog accompanied her everywhere, both around the stables and away from them. And if her dog wasn't welcome, then Petra simply didn't go there; like the fancy restaurant that had opened on the edge of the village, for instance. Not that she had any intention of eating there anyway, because she didn't. But if she'd had a mind to spend lots of money on tiny portions of food with ingredients she'd never heard of, the restaurant's dog-unfriendly ways would soon put her off.

Petra clipped a rope onto the goat's halter (god help it if a goat wasn't tethered, because the blighters were better escape artists than Houdini) and walked her across to a field. Hammering in a new stake, she tied Princess to it and let her loose on the brambles which were springing up in response to the increased levels of sunlight and the warmer weather.

As well as early mornings, Petra also loved the spring. All those fresh green shoots and sweet grass, the bluebells carpeting the woodlands, the primroses poking their heads out of the hedgerows – it was a lovely time of year. And she couldn't forget the tiny lambs, the busily nesting birds with demanding chicks to feed, and the calves on the farm next door. A pair of barn owls were nesting in the barn (funnily enough), she'd noticed, and the swallows were back; she'd spotted them swooping and diving yesterday evening as she was bringing the horses and ponies in from the field for possibly the last time this winter. It was time to let them stay outside overnight, now that the risk of bad weather had passed.

All except for Hercules, her pride and joy. He was too precious to leave outside overnight and risk him damaging himself. Not that he probably would, but he could be a bit feisty sometimes and lash out with his back legs if one of the others got too close. An ex-racehorse, he was high-spirited and high-maintenance, and she loved him all the more for it.

She heard a vehicle trundling along the lane long before she saw it (sound travelled further at this time of day) and she waited in the yard for the girls to show up. Faith and Charity were twins, and Petra guessed that if they had been part of a set of triplets, the third sister would have been called Hope.

They were as alike as two peas in a pod, and it had taken her a while to tell one from the other; but now that she could, the differences were obvious. Faith had a couple more freckles scattered across her nose than Charity had, and Charity sported a tiny scar on her cheek, courtesy of an encounter with some barbed wire. There were subtler differences, too, which Petra couldn't for the life of her describe but which she was aware of nevertheless, and altogether they added up to make the two girls distinct and separate.

But as far as personalities went, the sisters couldn't be more different; Faith was outgoing and the life and soul of the party, while Charity was shy and introverted. They did have one thing in common, though – their love of horses.

They'd been coming to the stable for years, ever since they were little and long before Petra had taken over from her great uncle, Amos. Amos was still around, but nowhere near as involved as he used to be – a heart problem had seen to that. These days he was content to let Petra get on with things (as long as she did them the way he used to, that is) and he spent his days pottering around doing the things he liked and was still able to manage.

Faith and Charity kept their own horses at the stables for free in exchange for their labour, and Petra didn't know what she'd do without them. She could only afford to pay one person and that was Nathan, whom she could hear whistling as he headed for the tractor. Today he was planning to fix the fence in the bottom field and the tractor's trailer was loaded up with posts and coiled lengths of wire.

'Morning,' she said, as the girls got out of Faith's bright yellow Beetle.

They were dressed, as was Petra, in green wellies, olive waxed cotton jackets and dark-coloured jodhpurs, every item old and worn, and utterly suitable for mucking out a succession of stables.

Methodically the two of them started at one end of the stables and worked their way along the stalls, whilst Petra jumped onto a pony and rode the mare bare-back, using only her legs and her body weight to steer her, as she took another couple of ponies to the field furthest from the house. To be fair to the ponies, they knew exactly where they were going, and they had a spring in their step as they half walked, half trotted, the scent of lush grass in their nostrils.

Petra slid off Beauty's back and opened the gate, the ponies almost pushing her aside in their eagerness to reach the new grazing, and she paused for a moment to watch them trot into the field, kicking up their legs and prancing. She waited until they settled down with their noses buried in the grass before walking back to fetch the next lot.

The sun was bright and there were only a few clouds in the sky, and it promised to be a nice day. Her breath misted in front of her as she strolled along the path, as it was still chilly at this time in the morning so early in the year, and she could see dew on the spiders' webs which were draped over the bushes on either side. A slight breeze ruffled her hair and she stopped to take in the view.

How she loved this place! She honestly couldn't imagine living anywhere else or doing anything else. She'd been horse mad since she was a child and had spent every waking moment she was allowed (and many when she wasn't) at these very stables. It had been the happiest day of her life when Amos had told her he wanted her to work for him.

That had been when she was nineteen, adrift with no real job to speak of, and no idea what she wanted to do with her life. Twelve years later, she was running the stables and was totally and utterly happy with her lot.

The animals were her life and she dedicated every waking minute to them. If she wasn't actively doing something with them or for them, then she was thinking about it, or planning it. And one had to be organised when one was responsible for running a stable, and she spent quite a lot of time planning weeks or months ahead. It wouldn't do to get to

November and realise that she was out of silage or hay, would it? By then it might be too late to buy any in, or the price might be sky-high, or the weather might be so bad that the delivery lorry wouldn't be able to get through. Planning ahead, being organised and having a routine was what she was all about. And right now her mind was on the annual gymkhana in the summer, as well as making sure the mucking out this morning was done to her satisfaction.

She'd just returned from another field, having dropped the remainder of the horses into it, and had come back for Hercules. He was a bit of a prima donna, and considerably more challenging than the rest of the equines in her stables. Unlike the three small ponies that she'd taken to share Princess's field, he didn't fare well on rough grass. They were content to nibble on the rough stuff. Hercules liked good-quality grass and she had to supplement his feed with oats and other grains, as well as hay.

'There's my lovely boy,' she called, seeing his rich chestnut head hanging over the lower door of his box. His ears pricked forward at the sound of her voice and he blew softly through his nose at her in greeting.

As she approached, he shuffled from foot to foot in anticipation, and when she finally got to him he thrust his head at her, butting her gently. She reached around his neck and put her arms around him, breathing in his familiar comforting horsey smell. He rested his chin on her shoulder and nibbled at her cheek, his soft hairy lips making her giggle.

'Get away with you,' she said, scratching between his ears.

They stayed in that position for a few minutes, until it became clear Hercules wanted his breakfast.

Petra went to fetch a full hay net and heaved it up onto the hook in the horse's stable. Then, while he was busy munching, tugging at the dried strands with his whiskery mobile lips, she checked him over, running her hands down his neck, over his shoulder and down his leg, picking up the hoof and checking it. She stroked his back, feeling the massive muscles of his hindquarters quiver at her touch, then her questing hands slid down his near-side hind leg and she did the same with that hoof. Then she moved around to his off-side and repeated the process.

Damn. He'd thrown a shoe on one of his front legs. It would probably be in the deep hay somewhere, but to be honest it wasn't worth hunting for. He was due a new set of shoes soon anyway, so she might as well have all four feet done at once.

With a resigned sigh, she gave the horse a final pat and went in search of her own breakfast.

'All set?' Ted asked, as Harry Milton opened the van door and sank into its saggy warmth. The van had seen better days and the springs on the passenger seat weren't as firm as they could be, but that was the least of Harry's worries.

He nodded at Ted, not feeling "all set" in the slightest. This was a big step for him.

Not the farrier part (he'd been shoeing horses for a good many years), but the buying a new business part and moving halfway across the country.

'We are going to Petra Kelly's stables first. Her stallion's thrown a shoe, but he'll probably need all four renewing. She's a tough bird. No nonsense. Don't expect any chit chat.'

Ted, Harry had discovered, was a man of few words himself, so Harry was grateful he was taking the time to share details of his clients with him. Soon though, they wouldn't be Ted's clients any longer; they'd be his. Of course, he'd have to earn them. They didn't come with the business, but Harry would take over Ted's round and hopefully Ted's clients would be happy with his work and would keep him on.

'Looking forward to retiring?' Harry asked, trying to make conversation.

'Nope. Gonna miss this.' Ted waved an arm at the scenery on the other side of the windscreen.

Harry had to admit that the patchwork of fields with the moorland above and the wooded valleys with streams running through them was a landscape a person could become very attached to. He was already falling in love with it, and he'd only been here two weeks. He'd moved to the area as soon as the sale of Ted's business had been agreed, and he couldn't wait to get started. There was one fly in the ointment though...

Harry tried to shy away from thoughts of Timothy; he needed to concentrate on work right now, not on his brother's problems, but it was hard not to focus on the worry that had consumed him ever since he'd fallen into the role of guardian when their parents had died so suddenly and so tragically. For the past fourteen years, he'd been both mother and father to Timothy. He still was and he didn't begrudge Timothy a single day of the love and care he'd lavished on him.

But for once, he was doing something for himself, and Timothy was old enough to decide what he wanted to do with his life. He'd decided to stay in the house they'd inherited from their parents. It was a sensible choice; his friends were there, his job was there, and so was his girlfriend. It was time Timothy stood on his own two feet, without Harry stifling him. He needed the space to grow into the adult he'd become, and Harry was aware that by living in the same house, the pair of them playing the same roles, he was holding his brother back. All Harry hoped, was that Timothy would be happy. Happiness was all he'd ever wanted for his little brother. His own was inconsequential.

Until, that is, he'd been flicking through a nag rag (one of the horsey newspapers) while attending a meet at Cheltenham Racecourse, and had spotted an advert for a farrier business for sale in the cutely named village of Picklewick. It was high time he branched out on his own, so he'd contacted Ted, and here he was, two months later, about to take over from Ted and begin a new chapter in his life.

'It is beautiful,' Harry agreed, especially with the landscape having a definite feel of spring in the air.

'Not that. I can see a field whenever I like. I'm gonna miss the freedom.' Ted

spoke the last word with deep feeling.
'The missus has already got stuff
planned.' His face fell into woebegone
folds, and Harry suppressed a smile. He
could empathise. He longed for freedom,
too.

'This is it,' Ted announced, hauling the
van's steering wheel to the right and
heading up a rough track towards a
cluster of buildings. Horses and ponies
grazed the fields either side of the pitted
track, and he wondered which one of
them they were here to shoe.

Nerves knotted his stomach – this was his
very first job, with his very first client. Ted
might be with him (he'd kindly offered to
accompany him for a couple of weeks to
introduce him and to vouch for him), but
Harry was under no illusion that he had to

step up to the mark, or risk losing everything.

Ted brought the van to a halt in a very clean-looking yard, and hopped out. He might be getting on in years, but you'd never know it, Harry thought, extricating himself from the seat with far less agility.

'Don't say nothing,' Ted said out of the corner of his mouth, even though there didn't appear to be anyone around. 'Leave the talking to me. She'll come round. Petra is a tough nut, but she loves her horses.'

Great. His first client sounded a right old battle-axe, and his stomach clenched tighter. Please let me get this right, he thought.

Then he gave himself a mental shake.

He could do this. He had been doing it; for years and years. He'd dealt with all manner of horses, from hideously expensive racehorses to the smallest of Pony Club mounts. He'd dealt with all manner of owners, too, and they had often proved to be more difficult than their animals.

He'd be fine. Wouldn't he?

CHAPTER TWO

Petra leant back in the saddle, one hand resting on her thigh, the other holding the reins loosely in order to allow the horse to pick her way over the rough track. Mabel was an elderly lady with a calming influence on the other ponies, who were all old hands themselves. They knew what they were doing, and what was expected of them, which allowed Petra to enjoy the hack rather than having to worry about her young charges. Easter was always a busy time for the stables, and especially this one what with the school holidays being late and the weather being so much better than earlier on in the year. Parents were happier letting their kids sit on the back of a pony for a couple of hours when they knew they wouldn't be blue with cold by the time they got back.

Petra, though, couldn't be choosy about when she rode, because the animals in her care needed exercising regardless of the weather conditions. But today was gorgeous, the early morning promise having been kept as dawn turned into mid-morning and the sun grew warm on her face as she turned it up to the sky.

Her body swaying gently to the rhythm of the mare's stride, Petra closed her eyes for a moment as she breathed in the scent of growing things, horse, and leather. It was better than any perfume, she thought, no matter how expensive. The clip and plod of the horses' hooves, along with the occasional snort and the creak of leather, provided an accompaniment to the orchestra of bird song and the rustle of little feathered bodies darting amongst the branches.

How could anyone prefer to work indoors on a day like today, she mused, shuddering at the thought of being confined to a desk in an air-conditioned office, unable to feel the breeze in her hair or listen to the sounds of nature. It was unnatural, that's what it was.

'Queenie, come here girl,' she called to the spaniel, who'd gone tearing off into the undergrowth, probably catching the scent of a rabbit or another small creature.

The dog returned to the horse's side, her tongue lolling and her tail wagging furiously.

Petra glanced behind her to check all was well, knowing it was from the steady plod of four sets of hooves and the occasional snort or shake of the head, but wanting to make sure anyway.

The ponies were in single file, practically nose to tail, appearing to be almost asleep, yet she knew they would respond in an instant if asked to do so. As soon as they came down off the hill and the terrain levelled out, she'd urge them into a canter. The final race for home was what her clients enjoyed the most, as the ponies made a controlled dash to the stable, anticipating a quick rub down after their tack was removed and then being released into the field.

Petra would bring them in again later for the early evening rides which were booked, but for the moment they'd be free to enjoy a long afternoon in the spring sunshine.

As soon as she thought it safe, she held Mabel back to allow the other ponies to walk ahead of her. Mabel, for all her advancing years, knew the score and as each pony trotted past, their ears pricked and their heads held high, she pranced and cavorted, as anxious as the rest of them. All the riders took off across the field, hanging onto the reins as they tried to control their mounts' speed, and Petra brought up the rear, prepared to intervene if anyone got into difficulties, only slowing when a gate hindered their progress.

Once through, there was a fast trot up the lane, then a clatter of hooves as all five animals skittered over the cobbles and across the yard.

Petra noticed that Ted's van was already there, and she nodded in satisfaction. Hercules would get his new set of shoes shortly and all would be well in his world.

All wasn't as it should be in hers however, as she spotted a stranger standing next to the farrier. He was possibly in his early to mid-thirties, tall, not bad looking if you liked clean-shaven, well-groomed men, and on her property when he had no right to be there. She wasn't expecting anyone and, come to think of it, how had he got here, because the only vehicles in the parking area were ones which were supposed to be there.

He could have walked, she conceded, but he didn't look the type to go for an aimless stroll around the countryside. His Wellington boots were too clean for a start. Despite the burgeoning spring weather, it was still muddy and slippery underfoot so if he had walked he'd stuck to the roads, and how boring was that!

She dismounted and handed her reins to Faith who came dashing out of the barn when she heard the clatter of hooves on cobbles, and walked over to the two men to find out what was going on.

'Morning,' Ted said. 'I'll fetch Hercules.' He nodded to her and stomped off in the direction of the horse's stall. A man of few words, Ted was better at dealing with equines than people. His age was indeterminable, although Petra suspected he was in his late sixties; his strength was undeniable (she'd seen him control a rearing horse which a lesser man would have had to have backed away from); and his patience was insurmountable –

with horses and other animals, that is.
With people, not so much.

Petra didn't mind. In fact, she liked it
because she knew where she stood with
him. He was down-to-earth and straight
to the point. Much like herself.

She waited for Ted to move out of
earshot, before turning to the stranger
and saying, 'Who are you and why are
you here? If you're trying to sell me feed
or wormers, I'm not interested.'

'I'm Harry Milton,' he replied, 'And I'm
taking over from Ted.'

Petra blinked at him, hoping she hadn't
heard correctly. 'You're doing what?'

'Ted is retiring and I'm taking over from
him.'

That might explain what he was doing in her yard and how he'd got here, but she wasn't happy about it. She hadn't any inkling that Ted was about to retire, and she didn't like the idea one little bit. She was used to Ted and he was used to her. He'd been shoeing her animals for years and he knew all their little foibles. What if this new bloke wasn't any good?

She wasn't sure she wanted to take the chance, but what choice did she have, other than to look around for another farrier. But if she did that, then she still wouldn't know if that one would be any good, either.

Darn it – she didn't like change. It didn't sit well with her.

But for the moment, she would have to put up with it, because Hercules needed shoes today, not in three months' time when she'd found someone suitable.

Petra glared at this new guy. 'He didn't tell me he was hanging up his horseshoes.'

'That's why I've accompanied him today, so I could meet his clients and introduce myself.'

Petra huffed. 'Are you any good?'

'I'll let you be the judge of that,' he said, as Ted emerged from a horsebox with Hercules on the end of a lead rope.

'I'd prefer Ted to shoe him,' Petra said as Harry stepped forward.

The man stopped and looked at her, his expression inscrutable. 'As you wish.'

'Right, young fella,' Ted said to the new man, as he tethered the horse to a nearby post. 'Take a look at him.'

'I'd prefer it if he didn't,' Petra said.

Ted raised his eyebrows. 'That's up to you, but if this 'un don't shoe him, the horse won't get done today.'

'Why ever not?'

'I've got a problem with my back.'

'Since when?' Petra was surprised; Ted had always seemed so fit and robust.

'For a while.'

'Is that why you're retiring?'

'Partly.'

'I see.'

'And then there's the missus,' he added.

'Oh?' She didn't know he was married; then again, why should she? The only things they ever talked about were horses, and the weather – and the latter was only discussed if it was unduly unusual.

'Harry will see you right,' Ted said.

'He will?' She still wasn't convinced.

'Aye.'

It appeared that was all Ted was prepared to say on the matter, as he closed his mouth and stared at her.

She'd have to take his word for it; at least Ted was here to supervise. He might not give a hoot about people, but he would never let anything happen to a horse.

Harry was conscious of Petra's eyes on him the whole time, from the second he approached the horse – murmuring softly to the animal and letting the horse sniff him before running his hands down each leg and lifting it to check the condition of the hooves – to shoeing the last foot, replacing it gently on the ground and giving the horse a pat on his solid rump.

'All done, fella,' he said. 'You were a good boy, weren't you?'

Hercules turned to look at him out of one eye and blew down his nose. His tail swished across Harry's face and he laughed. He could have sworn the horse was laughing too.

Petra wasn't. She looked as po-faced as when he'd first set eyes on her.

Ted had been watching closely as he worked, nodding now and again in what Harry hoped was approval. He knew he was good at his job; he'd worked with one of the best farriers in the country. So why did he feel as though he had just sat some kind of exam, which he wasn't entirely sure he'd passed.

He intercepted a look between Ted and Petra and almost jumped out of his skin when the woman said, 'You might as well meet the rest of my animals, while you're here. I don't want any work done on them today,' she added in a warning tone. 'They don't need it.'

'Go take a look, lad. I'll wait here.' Ted leant against the side of the van and folded his arms, so Harry obediently followed Petra, who was already halfway

across the yard, a black spaniel trotting
at her heels.

He hurried to catch up.

'I've got seventeen ponies, three horses, a
donkey and a goat. The goat is the only
one of those who doesn't need your
services.'

'I can take a look at it while I'm here?' he
offered.

Petra shot him a sharp glance. 'I can trim
her feet myself, thank you.'

'I'm sure you can—'

'Can I just say that I'm not happy Ted's
retiring,' she broke in. 'I get on well with
Ted. He doesn't bother me and I don't
bother him. He just gets on with his job.'

He'd gathered that she wasn't ecstatic he was here. He also gathered that she wasn't the friendliest of clients. He vowed to cause her as little bother as possible. He might need her custom and she might need his services, but that didn't mean they had to become bosom buddies.

The rest of his visit took place in silence, interspersed with the occasional stilted comment or brief question and answer, so Harry was glad when the tour was finally over and he could return to the far more garrulous and friendly Ted (and that was saying something!).

'I didn't realise you had a problem with your back,' Harry said, once they were on the road to the next job.

'I don't.'

'But you said—'

'I know what I said.' Ted chuckled. 'Worked, didn't it? And she'll accept you next time. Petra is a bit like a flighty filly being introduced to a stallion – she needs a firm hand.'

Harry's eyebrows rose. Never in a million years would he have compared Petra to a filly. Neither would he have called himself a stallion. He was more like a weary old carthorse and she was a stubborn mare.

He had to admit that she was rather attractive in a girl-next-door kind of way, with her make-up free face and honey-coloured hair gathered into a messy knot at the nape of her neck. She had arresting eyes, too – they were almond-shaped and green-blue in colour, and she'd used them to scrutinise him.

He wondered what she'd seen when she'd stared at him.

He wondered what she'd thought of him.

Then he shoved his wondering to one side. It didn't matter a jot as long as she thought he was professional, could do a good job and would use him on her animals again.

CHAPTER THREE

Petra stowed the pitchfork back in the tool shed and sighed deeply. It had been another tiring day. The days were all tiring lately, and she wondered if she was getting old. Thirty-one was hardly considered old, but she found she wasn't able to work for quite as long or quite as hard as she'd done when she had been in her twenties. It was as though a dial had been turned down a notch on her thirtieth birthday and it had yet to be turned back up.

'I've bedded the terrible twosome down,' Charity said, appearing from behind the stable block. 'Is there anything else before I go?'

The terrible twosome was a pair of Shetland ponies who refused to go anywhere without each other. If only one was needed for a ride, the other had to go too, albeit riderless. Petra knew she should try to loosen their dependency on each other, but what harm was it doing? She didn't mind, and if it made the little creatures happy then who was she to separate them.

'No, you get off, thanks,' she said. 'How are you fixed for taking a trek out on Saturday for a couple of hours? I wouldn't normally ask but I've got that kiddies' party booked in, and this is for seven people, so...'

She knew Charity would pick up on the subtext — a booking for seven people for

a two-hour trek was a substantial amount
of money when every penny counted.
Running a riding stables wasn't cheap,
which was why Petra was branching out
into other activities, such as pony parties,
where children could enjoy all the fun of a
birthday party combined with horsey
games.

'I'm working, but I'll ask Faith. I think
she's got this weekend off.'

'Thanks, love.'

Petra watched the girl head for her car
and sighed. Faith and Charity were hardly
girls anymore, although they had been
when they'd first started stabling their
horses with her. She'd watched them
grow from awkward teenagers into the
charming young women they were today.
Not only did it make her feel old, it also
worried her – she depended on their help

so much that she didn't know what she'd do if marriage and babies eclipsed their love of horses. And it was bound to happen – husbands and children took up so much time and attention, it was inevitable that once the twins settled down they wouldn't be able to be at the stables as much. They might even decide to sell their horses.

The thought horrified her. It was bad enough when an animal died (she recalled how heartbroken she'd been when Prince dropped dead last year – it was from old age and he'd had a long and wonderful life, but the knowledge didn't ease the hurt), but to actively move a horse to a new home went totally against the grain as far as Petra was concerned. She simply couldn't imagine doing such a thing.

Although to be fair, she couldn't imagine
having a husband or children either. And
neither did she want to. She had
everything she needed right here. Besides,
she didn't have the time for love. Human
love, that is. She had all the love in the
world for her animals.

As if sensing her thoughts, Fred stalked
up to her and pecked her boot.

'Yes, I know, it's time you and your ladies
were tucked up in bed,' she told the
cockerel, who was strutting around her
feet making soft little noises of
contentment.

Fred had a great deal to be contented
about, Petra thought, as she rounded up
the hens and shepherded them into the
coop for the night. They were allowed to
wander at will during the day, and with
plenty of food, all that grubbing around

and fresh air, they had perfect lives for chickens. That perfection filtered through to the wonderfully tasting eggs they laid.

'You reap what you sow,' she murmured to herself as she ensured the lock was securely fastened, and she smiled as she heard the pre-bed squabbling taking place inside. Each bird might roost in the same place every night, but it didn't stop them having a tiff about it. Chickens tended to enjoy a good squabble.

After a final check around with Queenie at her heels, Petra finally headed to the house, her supper and Amos.

'Finished for the day?' her uncle called from the kitchen when he heard her enter the boot room.

Petra smiled. He always asked the same thing. 'Yep, everyone is in bed,' she shouted back, easing her wellies off and wriggling her toes. Queenie shook herself and clambered into her basket, snuggling up to Tiddles, who was already there.

The grey cat gave Queenie a narrow-eyed stare, but allowed the dog to join her in the basket. It might belong to Queenie but as far as the cat was concerned she had squatters' rights and it was first come, first served.

'Anything I can do?' Amos asked this question every evening, too. One day she'd surprise him and suggest something. He'd probably like that, she thought, but he had enough on his plate these days with keeping the house going and staying on top of the accounts. His days of hauling bales of hay around were long gone.

'What's for supper?' she asked, sniffing appreciatively. She'd never been much of a cook, but that didn't mean she didn't enjoy food, especially when someone else prepared it for her.

'Lamb chops, with roast potatoes and the last of the carrots.' Amos had a small veggie plot at the back of the house and he took great pride in providing fresh food for the table whenever he could. The carrots had been overwintered in the root cellar, a leftover from when the stables had been a working farm many moons ago.

The pair of them ate their meal whilst discussing the events of the day.

'Ted retiring!' Amos exclaimed when she told him the news. 'Well, I never. He kept that quiet. He brought a new guy with him, you say?'

'Yes, a young chap. He seemed to know what he was doing though.' Petra still wasn't sure about Harry, but time would tell, and the fact that Ted was vouching for him gave her some confidence.

'How young?'

'Early thirties.'

Amos spluttered. 'When you said "young" I thought you meant a teenager.'

'He might as well be one – it'll be a long time before he's got Ted's experience. He shoed Hercules okay, though,' she added grudgingly.

'What's his name?'

'Harry Milton.'

'What's he like?'

'I told you – younger than I'd like him to be.'

'Does it matter how old he is, as long as he knows what he's doing?'

Petra shrugged. 'I suppose not.'

'What's he like?' Amos repeated.

'Not bad looking, tall, broad-shouldered...' She trailed off. 'What?'

'I meant, what's he like with the horses.' Her uncle gave her a quizzical look and Petra blushed, the heat creeping up her neck and into her cheeks.

'Oh, I see, um, good. He was good. Hercules liked him.' What on earth had got into her? Of course Amos wouldn't have wanted to know what Harry looked like. His looks, good or otherwise, were irrelevant.

Amos was still staring at her oddly. 'What?' she demanded irritably.

'You like him, don't you?'

'I do not!'

'Hmm.'

'Don't "hmm" me. I told you, I don't like him.'

'You think he's good-looking – you just said so.'

Petra stuck her nose in the air and refused to answer.

'I miss your Aunt Mags,' he said out of the blue, and Petra immediately softened.

'I know you do,' she said, reaching across the table to lay her hand on top of his. She was well aware he missed her. How

could he not, when her aunt and uncle
had been together for so long. Her death
had been a blow to everyone. And no
matter that it had happened years ago,
Petra could vividly recall how upset she
had been, so she couldn't even imagine
what her uncle must have gone through.
Was still going through.

'Don't leave it too late,' he said.

Confused, Petra asked, 'Leave what too
late?'

'Finding love. It's the only thing that truly
matters. If you spend your life alone,
you'll miss out on so much.' His eyes were
glossy with unshed tears, and Petra felt
close to crying herself. Not because she
didn't have a man in her life (she neither
wanted one, nor needed one) but because
her uncle was still in so much pain at the
loss of his wife. If there was something –

anything – she could do to alleviate even a fraction of the hurt he was feeling, she'd do it in a heartbeat.

'I'm fine as I am, Amos.' She was. She didn't need a man to complete her; she was already complete. Running the stables and being with horses all day was all she'd ever wanted, and she considered herself truly blessed. She had enough people to love – well, horses, although she obviously loved Amos, and she cared deeply for Nathen, Faith and Charity. Anyone else would only be a distraction and a hindrance.

'You're past thirty,' Amos pointed out. 'Don't leave it too late.'

'Thirty isn't old,' Petra scoffed. 'And I'm only just gone thirty.'

Amos pounced. 'Ha! So you are open to love.'

'No! Didn't I just say so?' He was trying to trip her up with this convoluted way of thinking, but she wasn't having any of it.

Her uncle smiled sadly. 'Petra, my sweet, I'm serious. Everyone needs a special someone in their life. It's high time you found yours.'

Petra rolled her eyes, and instead of responding to his ridiculousness she got to her feet and began clearing the table.

Why, oh why, though, did the image of the new farrier pop into her mind?

Harry relaxed into his sofa with a deep sigh, a bottle of ice-cold beer in his hand,

and he thought about the day he'd just had.

All in all, he thought it had gone quite well. Aside from making necessary visits to those clients who Ted had been scheduled to see, they'd also made the odd detour or two to pop in on a few other locals so that Ted could introduce him and explain he was taking over the business.

Most people, especially those whose animals he had tended to, were sad to see Ted go, but seemed happy enough that Harry was taking over.

There was only one person who still appeared to have reservations about him after he'd done his job (under Ted's watchful eye, of course) and that was Petra.

What was her problem? He'd shown he was more than capable, so what more did she want from him? Ted had told him that she didn't like change, but that was tough – change happened all the time. And him replacing Ted was hardly a major one. He'd only see her a few times a year, even with him living in the nearest village to the stables. Muddypuddle Lane was over a mile long, and the stables were at the far end of it. He might bump into her occasionally in Picklewick, but on the other hand she might prefer to do her shopping further afield. Either way, his arrival could hardly be described as a life-changing event for her.

So, he asked himself again, what was her problem?

Maybe it was him, personally. She might have taken an instant dislike to him, for some reason. He didn't think he was a particularly unlikeable bloke, but he supposed it was possible. You heard of love at first sight – so maybe Petra had experienced hate at first sight the second she clapped eyes on him, though perhaps "hate" was too strong a word.

Oh well, he thought, you can't please all the people all the time, and if the only client who was displeased with him was Petra, he could live with that. It would be a shame if she took her custom elsewhere, though; she was by far one of the biggest clients in his patch. Maybe he could reduce his rates for her, a kind of bulk buy thing. Or maybe not – margins were tight as they were, without making them worse.

He'd have a think, see how things went. It could be that they would agree not to like each other and he could still retain her as a client.

He paused as a thought struck him; he didn't dislike her in return, and he wasn't referring to the fact that he found her attractive either (although she undoubtedly was). And that was quite odd – to like someone when they didn't like you.

Harry took another swig of his beer, his head beginning to ache with all the second-guessing he was doing, and he deliberately dragged his thoughts away from Petra and her stables, and directed them to his cottage. He had taken out a six-month lease on it with the idea that he'd settle into the area first before he thought about buying. Although, if he was honest, this little cottage with its three outbuildings was perfect. He didn't need any more than two bedrooms (one for him and one for Timothy when he came for a visit) and the larger the place, the more there was to clean. He preferred outdoor spaces, and this cottage had an enchanting garden backing onto a field in which a pair of horses grazed.

He ran his eye over them, automatically noting their configuration and their general state of health. Their coats shone in the last rays of the setting sun as they cropped the grass, and the scene was one of peace and contentment.

Harry had considered sitting outside this evening but it was still rather early in the year, and once the sun dropped lower in the sky, winter's chill returned as if reluctant to let go and admit defeat.

Movement caught his eye and he watched as a woman strode across the field, a bucket in one hand and a couple of lead ropes in the other. Her voice calling to the horses carried faintly through the window, and Harry wondered if Petra had brought her animals in for the night yet.

Then he frowned because he didn't want to think about her right now, so why had she popped into his thoughts again?

The horses had gone to the woman willingly enough, their heads pushing at her as both of them tried to stick their noses in the bucket she held, and Harry smiled. He hadn't ridden in a long time. Too long. Maybe that was why he kept thinking about Petra and her stables – he should book a hack with her. It would be good to ride again, and hacking in the hills around the village would help him explore the area.

And you never know, he said to himself as he finished his beer, she might even begin to like him a little bit. Although why that should matter to him, he hadn't the slightest idea.

CHAPTER FOUR

Petra was rather touched to be invited to Ted's retirement party. She hadn't thought they were all that close, but when she climbed the stairs to the function room on the first floor of the Black Horse and saw how many people had turned up to wish him well, she didn't feel quite so special. Still, it was nice to see that the residents of Picklewick and the surrounding area thought so highly of the old farrier. All she hoped was that the new one would be as good at his job.

She had no reason to believe that Harry wouldn't be, and he'd done a competent enough job on Hercules – she'd checked the horse's hooves after Ted and Harry left. It was just that she was used to Ted, and he was used to her. She'd get used to this new one eventually, of course she would.

As though thinking about the new farrier had conjured him into being, she spotted him at the bar and she quickly turned away before he realised she'd noticed him. There were far too many people at this party who'd expect her to chat with them as it was, without throwing his name into the hat. People like the glamorous and opinionated Cher, whose daughter Thaila (pronounced Taylor – Petra had been told the first time she'd met the child, who was as precocious as her mother) used to have riding lessons every week until Petra told her where to stick her suggestions. Cher had always wanted to chat – and although "chat" was the word Cher used, Petra thought "harangue" was a far more accurate description of what actually passed between them. She pitied Thaila's teachers, but she pitied the owner of the riding school Thaila now attended, even more.

Oh dear, Cher had spotted her and was heading in her direction.

Petra hastily swallowed what was left of her wine and using the need for a top-up as an excuse, waved her empty glass at the woman bearing down on her and dashed to the bar, only to find herself next to another person she wasn't too keen on engaging in conversation with this evening. She was beginning to wish she hadn't come.

'Harry,' she said. It sounded more like an accusation than a greeting, and she tried to temper it with a friendly nod.

He appeared to be amused. A small smile played about his lips and his eyes crinkled a little at the corners. He scrubbed up well, she noticed. The old jeans and hoodie had been replaced with charcoal chinos and a white button-down shirt with the sleeves rolled up, showing his muscular forearms. Petra looked away.

'Nice to see you again,' he said politely. 'How is Hercules?'

'He's very well, thank you.' She'd ridden him several times since he'd been shod and she hadn't been aware of any issues. 'I rode him today, in fact,' she added, as though Harry had been privy to her thoughts.

'I've been meaning to ask you...I'd like to go out on a hack sometime.'

Petra blinked. 'Um, okay,' she stuttered, then she pulled herself together and rallied. 'I'll have to assess your riding ability first,' she told him sharply. 'I can't have any old Tom, Dick or Harry—' She halted and bit her lip.

Harry, she saw, was trying not to laugh.

'What's so funny?' Cher's voice inserted itself into the conversation, quickly followed by the rest of her as she pushed her way between them.

Petra took a step back.

'So, you're the new farrier, are you? Ted has told me **aaalll** about you,' Cher drawled, and Petra watched her scan Harry from the tip of his loafers to the top of his dark hair. Petra could tell that the other woman clearly liked what she was seeing.

She took another step back, hoping to slip away unnoticed.

No such luck.

'Petra, aren't you going to introduce us?' Cher demanded. She did a lot of demanding, did Cher. And she was perfectly capable of introducing herself. Did the woman think she was living in the nineteenth century?

Sullenly Petra replied, 'Harry, meet Cher. Cher meet Harry. Now, if you'll excuse me, I have people to see.'

'No problem, run along,' Cher said, waving her hand dismissively, her attention on Harry. Petra could almost see the drool coming out of those too-red lips.

Petra "ran", but not before she caught a glimpse of the pleading look on Harry's face as she left.

Ha! She thought, serves him right.

Although, what it served him right for, she didn't have the faintest idea. She felt a twinge of guilt at abandoning him to deal with Cher on his own, but she pushed the feeling away by telling herself that all was fair in love and war, and when it came to Cher Reynolds, it most definitely **was** war.

'Sorry,' she mouthed at him before turning away and disappearing into the crowd, and in a way she was sorry. Not because she was leaving him in the tender care of a woman like Cher (she had no doubt

Harry could take care of himself) but that he might find the woman attractive.

Cher was a single mother, and she made it clear she wasn't averse to changing that status.

Petra fervently hoped Cher didn't get to change her single status by netting Harry Milton. And by that, she only meant that she couldn't abide the idea of her new farrier being married to a woman she actively disliked and who, she suspected, had bad-mouthed her stables on more than one occasion.

No wonder she preferred horses to people, Petra thought as she smiled a greeting to the parents of a little lad by the name of Simon who loved horses as much as she did. You knew where you were with horses. People were far trickier.

But every now and then, throughout the
evening, she couldn't help her gaze
seeking out Harry to check that he wasn't
as interested in Cher as Cher clearly
hoped he would be.

Harry was not amused. He'd spent most
of the party trying to avoid that Cher-
woman who Petra had introduced him to.
He could have sworn Petra had been
laughing at him as she slipped away,
using the flimsy excuse that she had other
people to speak to.

Not that he particularly wanted Petra to
stay and talk to him (he didn't), he simply
hadn't wanted to be left alone with Cher.
The woman scared him – she'd kept
putting her hand on his arm and leaning
too close so her perfume made his eyes
water.

When he'd eventually escaped, saying he needed the loo, her eyes had been on his back (he could feel them boring into him) as he weaved his way to the door. He'd washed his hands, spent a few minutes giving himself a mental talking to, then had sidled back into the party hoping his entrance would go unnoticed.

His tactics hadn't worked. Cher had positioned herself near the door, and she spotted him as soon as he reappeared; it was only Ted wanting him to meet someone that saved him from an evening of being hounded.

As soon as he was free of Cher's clutches, he looked for Petra, hoping to tease her about her abandonment of him, but he couldn't see her.

He didn't see her for the rest of the party, and when he put his weary self to bed

later that night his thoughts had filled
with all the new people he'd met, but the
only image to stay with him as he drifted
off to sleep was that of Petra mouthing
"sorry" at him, and the twinkle in her eye
as she abandoned him to his fate.

CHAPTER FIVE

Not even her beloved Hercules could lift Petra's mood. She'd been as grumpy as a badger with a snout full of bee stings ever since Ted's retirement party on Friday night, and she had no idea why.

She could try to blame it on having a Sunday filled with back-to-back lessons, followed by a trek with a group of giggling teenage girls who had spent as much time looking at their phones as they had in paying attention to their mounts until she was sick of yelling at them to pull their ponies' heads out of the verges.

She couldn't blame the ponies for taking the opportunity to snatch at the grass – after all, equines were eating machines, spending up to sixteen hours a day grazing if left to their own devices. However, she didn't leave them to their own devices; she expected them to work for their hay and grain, and too much rich grass could lead to all kinds of problems, especially when it came to a greedy creature like Tango, a cob who was prone to laminitis if she didn't watch him.

She made a mental note to pop a grazing muzzle on him before she turned him out into the field. It didn't prevent him from grazing, but it limited his intake of grass and made him work harder for it. He hated wearing it, but Petra knew it was better than trying to treat any resulting laminitis. As well as the pain the horse would be in, laminitis meant numerous visits by both the vet and the farrier as they tried to treat the swelling of the hoof and the bone. The vet was expensive, and she was already seeing far more of the farrier than she wanted to.

By the time she'd arrived back at the stables and the girls had left, she was in a foul mood. Wrestling with Tango didn't help, as he kept tossing his head in annoyance and his nose had dealt her a glancing blow on the chin, making her yelp in pain.

'Tango!' she shouted at him, and he glared at her balefully, eyeing the muzzle with dislike. 'It's for your own good.'

Eventually she managed to slip it over his nose and buckle the strap behind his ears. Then she smiled gently at the sad expression on his face.

Bless him. He looked awfully sorry for himself.

His expression mirrored her own she noticed, as she caught sight of her reflection in one of the old farmhouse windows a short while later, and she couldn't believe how glum she looked.

Snap out of it, she told herself. She had nothing to be miserable about; the stables were doing well (she'd never be rich, but the income was steady), she had a job she loved, and she was happy (wasn't she? – of course she was).

What more could she possibly want?

When Harry's face popped into her mind, she angrily shoved it away. He had no right to invade her thoughts and she had a good mind to tell him so. And she would too, apart from the fact that she didn't want to admit that he seemed to have taken up residence in her head.

Okay, she admitted reluctantly, he was damned attractive, but handsome is as handsome does as the old saying goes, and no good would come of it. Look at the problems he had with Cher. That woman was a man-eater if ever there was one. She made no secret that she was hunting for a husband, and at one point she had set her sights on a locum doctor. Now she appeared to be targeting the new farrier.

Petra's one consolation was her memory of the wide-eyed helpless stare he'd sent her as she'd left him to Cher's tender mercies. Harry's discomfort had cheered her up no end.

'Have you got the number for the new farrier?' Faith asked Petra a couple of days later. 'Midnight has thrown another shoe. I honestly don't know how he does it.' She grimaced. 'I'm beginning to think he's doing it on purpose; like he's in his stable every night, working out how to prise them off.'

Petra laughed. How long horses kept shoes on their hooves depended on a variety of factors such as how fast the hoof grew, what terrain the horse walked on, or overreaching by the hind feet.

Midnight was notorious for losing his.

'Yes, it's on the wall in the office, above the phone. Have you found the shoe?' Sometimes the horseshoe could be found in a field or a stable, but more often than not it simply disappeared. And even if it was found, it couldn't always be reused.

'Not yet.' Faith heaved a sigh. 'He's costing me a fortune.'

Petra sympathised. Owning a horse was expensive and riding wasn't a cheap hobby. Which was why the arrangement she had with Faith and her twin to house their horses at the stables for free in exchange for help around the place, suited all three of them. Including the horses, who were sometimes used for lessons and hacks if either of the twins didn't have time to exercise their animals.

Apart from throwing his shoes on a regular basis, Midnight was a sweet fella, and Petra had a soft spot for him. 'I'll see if I can find it after I've sorted the others out,' she said, knowing that the girl had to go to work. 'It can't have gone far.'

Which were famous last words, she thought sometime later as she was rooting through the straw on the stable floor. It wasn't quite like looking for a needle in a haystack because a cast shoe was a fairly substantial item, but it certainly felt like it.

'Is he in one of the fields?' a man's voice called, making her jump.

She straightened up and whirled around to see Harry leaning against the door, watching her.

Great. He'd had a perfect view of her backside as she'd been scrabbling around on the floor.

'In the bottom one,' she muttered, then instantly regretting using the word "bottom". In a rare display of embarrassment, she felt heat flood into her cheeks. This was the second time this man had made her blush. Cross with herself, she added briskly, 'Can you find it on your own, or do you need some help?'

'I dare say I can manage. Which horse is it?'

'Midnight.' She was about to describe the horse when Harry spoke.

'Ah, dark brown, sixteen hands, gelding,' he said.

Petra raised her eyebrows.

'I paid attention when you showed me around.'

She was impressed. Although she tended to remember horses better than people, she was aware most folks weren't like that.

'Besides,' he added with a grin. 'If I couldn't work out which animal in the field had lost a shoe, I wouldn't be much of a farrier, would I? So you can carry on doing what you're doing – I'll fetch him myself.'

His smile was infectious, and she found her lips curving upwards in response. Hastily, she dropped the smile; she didn't want him to think she was interested in him. She didn't want to come across like Cher did, all giggles and dimpled cheeks. The blushing was bad enough, but at least she could put that down to straightening up suddenly. Not that he'd mentioned it; but if he did...

'Right then,' he said. 'I'll get on. Is he wearing a halter?'

Guilt pricked at her – it wasn't a farrier's job to go chasing around a field after a horse. The animal should be ready and waiting. 'I'll get him,' she said, and he stood aside to let her pass.

'I may as well come with you,' he suggested, and she couldn't think of a reason not to let him. Actually, she could, but she wasn't prepared to share with him the information that he made her uncomfortable.

Not uncomfortable, exactly. More...out of sorts. She couldn't describe it to herself, so trying to explain it to the man striding down the track next to her would be difficult. She was far too aware of his nearness for her liking. She could see his profile out of the corner of her eye, she could smell the subtle scent of him – citrus and fresh – and she could almost feel the warmth of his arm as it swung by his side, matching her pace for pace.

Suddenly aware that she was practically running along the path leading to the field, she slowed a little, feeling slightly breathless. Which was odd because she was extremely fit. A bit of walking shouldn't make her heart beat faster, or her pulse throb in her ears, and neither should she feel as though she couldn't catch her breath.

Maybe she was coming down with something? If so, it would be a damned inconvenience that she could do without. Surreptitiously she felt her forehead, hoping she didn't have the beginnings of a temperature. But although she was feeling all hot and bothered, her brow was cool enough.

Thank goodness for that. She was far too busy to be ill, and she knew she was a horrid patient. But her lack of a temperature didn't explain why she was feeling so odd.

Petra left Harry at the gate whilst she went into the field to catch Midnight, which was easier said than done as the horse had only been turned out a couple of hours ago and didn't fancy being brought back in because it usually meant he had to do some work.

She caught him eventually and led him to Harry who, she saw, was gazing intently at them. Yet another blush threatened to flood her cheeks at his scrutiny, and she willed her body to behave. This was becoming quite ridiculous. She was regressing into a teenager with a first crush.

Her eyes widened and she came to a stop.

That's what was wrong with her! She was behaving like a filly faced with a handsome stallion (not that fillies gave a hoot for a stallion's looks), and she gave herself a mental shake. How absurd, her having a crush on the new farrier. She wasn't behaving any better than Cher, but at least Cher was being honest with herself and with the man she fancied. Harry knew where he stood with Cher.

'Everything okay?' he called, and she jumped, her sudden movement making Midnight toss his head in annoyance.

'Fine. Sorry, miles away for a minute.' She carried on walking as he opened the gate and led the horse through it.

'I was watching him as you brought him up the field and apart from the cast shoe, he looks a little lame in his nearside back leg, to me,' Harry said, and Petra suppressed a groan.

He hadn't been studying her at all – he had been examining the horse. Of course he had – that was **why** he was there.

Feeling incredibility foolish, she carried on walking without saying anything until they reached the usual place where she hitched any horses who were about to be shod.

She tied Midnight up then headed back to the house, calling over her shoulder, 'Let Faith know what you find. You can leave him there when you've finished – I'll see to him later.'

Ignoring the eyes she could feel on her back, she marched across the yard, darted into the house and as soon as she was safely out of sight, collapsed into a chair and rubbed a slightly shaking hand across her face.

Dear god, she didn't need this. She didn't need him, or any other man for that matter. She was happy as she was; but even as she told herself that, she could sense the doubt in the back of her mind asking if she truly was happy, or whether she'd said it so often she had come to believe it.

When she heard the sound of Harry's van pulling out of the yard sometime later, she finally looked up to see Amos staring. She hadn't heard him come in and he was sitting in one of the other chairs. How long he'd been there she had no idea, and she wondered what he was making of her strange behaviour this morning.

Then he said, 'Don't leave it too late,' and she knew precisely what he was thinking.

And she also knew precisely what she was going to do with his advice.

Ignore it.

Because she was happy just the way she was.

CHAPTER SIX

Mondays, Ted had informed Harry before he'd handed over the reins of the business to him for good, tended to be busy. Horses and ponies were ridden more at the weekends and owners tended to notice thrown shoes more, and they all wanted their animals seen to as soon as possible. For Harry, weekends had always been business as usual as he'd often attended races as the on-site farrier. It was a welcome change to have weekends off, although he was still on call in an emergency. So far, no one had needed him and everything had been routine.

Today he was attending a stable some thirteen miles from Picklewick. Several animals were due to be re-shoed (every six weeks for working horses was quite common) and he'd set aside a chunk of time to do just that. He'd just finished and was stowing his equipment in the back of Ted's (now his) van, when he saw a familiar figure trotting towards him.

It was Cher, and his heart sank.

'Harry? I thought it was you.' She tottered over to him in heels far too high to be worn in a stable yard. 'What are you doing here?' she asked, then she put a hand to her mouth and gave a tinkling giggle. 'Silly me. You're working.'

'Yes, I am,' he agreed.

She stared at him and he realised he was supposed to ask her what she was doing here in return. He didn't. Instead, he told her, 'I've got to get on; another job to go to.'

'I was hoping to bump into you,' she said, laying a hand on his arm. 'I wanted to ask you something.'

'Oh?' His mind whirled with possibilities and he dreaded what she was about to ask. She'd come on to him fairly heavily the other night and he knew she'd been flirting outrageously with him.

'I need your advice and your help,' she said.

'What with?' His reply was cautious.

'Can we have a chat about it some other time? I've got to pick Thaila up from school and you've said you've got a job to go to.'

'Um, okay.'

'How about we meet for coffee? I can do tomorrow.'

His curiosity piqued, Harry said, 'Lunchtime?' He had a couple of things on in the morning, but he had set the afternoon aside to work on his accounts, starting as he meant to go on, although he wasn't entirely convinced he'd keep his good intentions up. A quick coffee would split the day up.

'Lunch it is!' Cher twinkled at him.

He'd never seen anyone twinkle before, but he'd definitely been twinkled at. And he was sure he hadn't agreed to lunch, not in the way Cher was implying.

'We can go to the Black Horse, if you like?' This time she simpered, and he bit his lip. Her frivolous behaviour might appeal to another man but he was a more down-to-earth guy, and he found her a bit over the top. Petra was more his type.

His eyes widened as the thought took him by surprise.

'Or maybe not,' Cher said, seeing his expression. 'Let's avoid temptation, shall we?'

'Temptation?' he repeated blankly, his attention on the silly notion he'd just had. Petra wasn't his type at all – she was too grumpy for a start.

'Ooh, you naughty thing!' Cher tapped him on the arm in mock admonishment. 'I was referring to drinking at lunchtime.'

Harry hadn't been referring to anything at all, and now he was slightly bewildered and very much regretting agreeing to meet her.

'Let's go to Blake's Café in Picklewick,' she continued. 'They do some fantastic open sandwiches, or homemade soup if you prefer. Or maybe both – in your line of work you need to keep your strength up.' She eyed him up and down and he resisted the urge to squirm like a small boy needing the loo.

'Indeed,' he said, not knowing how else to respond.

'Shall we say twelve-thirty?'

'Fine. See you there,' he said, lifting his rolled-up bag of tools into the van and closing the door.

'I'll look forward to it,' Cher said, her smile revealing dimples in both of her cheeks.

Harry smiled back and gave her a wave of acknowledgment as he climbed into the van. He had to admit that she was an attractive woman, and she obviously took care of herself and had pride in her appearance. She wore the kind of make-up that made it appear she had hardly any on (he'd learnt that from one of Timothy's many girlfriends), her hair was glossy and bounced on her shoulders whenever she moved her head, and she had a good figure.

But when he compared her to the girl-next-door freshness and lithe frame of the owner of the stables on Muddypuddle Lane, he knew which woman he preferred.

It was just a pity Petra Kelly wasn't as interested in him as Cher Reynolds was.

He froze, his hand on the gear stick.

Why was Petra's lack of interest in him such a pity? What—?

Cher tapped on the glass and waved to him, pulling him out of his thoughts. He waggled his fingers at her, started the engine and hurriedly made his escape.

As he made his way to his next appointment, his mind was churning.

By the time he pulled into a field where a fellow with a massive Shire horse was waiting for him, hooves larger than serving platters, he'd arrived at the conclusion that he wanted to see more of Petra Kelly and it wasn't because of her equine charges, either.

She, however, hadn't shown the slightest inclination that she wanted to see any more of him. Quite the opposite, as her behaviour last week had shown.

The realisation was rather disappointing.

The following day Harry spotted Cher as he neared the café. She was sitting by the window and was watching out for him because the second she saw him she waved and beckoned for him to hurry up. He frowned a little – he wasn't late, he was early, because he'd been hoping to arrive before her so he could get his bearings.

Cher unsettled him. Not in a good way like Petra (stop thinking about her, he told himself) but in a "please-get-me-out-of-here" way, and he was anxious to hear what she had to say so he could leave. His plan was to have a half-drunk cup of coffee already in front of him, so as soon as she'd discussed what she wanted to discuss, he could make his excuses and dash off. However, she'd scuppered his plan, and now he was forced to sit through the ordering process, the wait for their orders to arrive and the imbibing of them, and all the while he simply knew she'd flirt.

She looked so pleased to see him when he sidled past the other tables to get to the one she was sitting at, that he immediately felt guilty. It wasn't her fault that she wasn't his type he thought, as Petra's pretty but scowling face appeared in his mind – Petra was the only woman he'd met who had piqued his interest since he'd moved to Picklewick.

Okay, more than pique, he admitted as he smiled politely at Cher and took a seat.

'You're early!' she exclaimed with pleasure, and he felt himself deflate even further.

Dear god, please don't let her think it was because he couldn't wait to see her. He didn't want her to get the wrong end of the stick, and he wasn't the type to lead her on.

'Sorry,' he said.

'Don't be.' She glanced quickly around, her gaze coming back to rest on his face. 'This is nice, isn't it? The two of us having lunch together.'

'Just a cup of coffee for me, I think,' he said, calling the waitress over, and he felt a right heel when Cher's face fell. He should never have agreed to meet with her today. Or any other day, for that matter. 'What advice do you need?' He decided to cut to the chase and get this over with before he upset her further.

'Oh yes, right. Um, Thaila wants a pony. She's been riding since she was three and she's been nagging for a horse for simply ages. I had said no, but her father – we're no longer together – has said he'll buy it for her. But he doesn't know the first thing about horses, so I told him that I'd have to choose it for her.' She put a hand on her chest, the varnish on her long nails shimmering. 'I'm no expert when it comes to horseflesh, although I do know more than my ex-husband, so I was hoping you could help?'

Harry pulled a face. 'I know about hooves and legs,' he said, 'but I'm not as hot on the rest of the animal.'

'Don't be so modest,' she giggled. 'I bet you know a pretty filly when you see one.' She fluttered her eyelashes.

Repressing a grimace, Harry said, 'I really wouldn't like to influence any decision you might make.'

'I won't hold it against you – not unless you ask me to,' she added with another suggestive giggle.

Crumbs, she was laying it on thick, making sure he knew she fancied him. 'I don't think I can help you,' he said, meaning he was certain he couldn't.

'Come with me then, for moral support.'

'I've got a better idea,' he said, suddenly struck with inspiration. 'Why don't you ask Petra?'

Cher's expression hardened. 'I don't think so. If she were the only person in the world who could tell one end of a horse from another, I still wouldn't ask her.'

'Oh.'

'Thaila had to move riding stables because of her.'

'Oh,' he repeated, not wanting to hear any more, and hoping Cher would take the hint.

'Petra Kelly is the rudest person on the planet. All I did was make a couple of suggestions which, I might add, would have made the whole riding lesson experience better for the grown-ups and she shot me down in flames. So rude.'

'I see.'

'Good. So then, will you come with me?'

'What were your suggestions?'

'Oh, um, some central heating in the indoor arena for the mums – it's mostly mums who have to sit through the lessons – a comfy sofa or two. Just little things to make the wait more bearable. It's so cold in the winter and those plastic chairs are awful. It's like being back in school.'

Harry barked out a laugh. Central heating, indeed? Sofas? Did the woman not realise that the arena was a converted barn and any heat would immediately leak out? And as for a sofa, plastic chairs were ideal because they could be washed down easily and they wouldn't rot.

'I know, right?' she carried on, mistaking his laugh for agreement. 'You still haven't answered my question. Please say you'll come.'

'Sorry, no. I don't think it's a good idea. Let me get these,' he added as their waitress approached with a tray. He took a note out of his wallet and handed it to the woman after she placed their drinks on the table. Then he rose. 'I've got to run. Sorry I can't help.'

And with that he hastened out of the café as fast as he could and drove home as though the hounds of hell were after him.

Petra hoisted her bag onto her shoulder yet again. It kept slipping down her arm and was starting to annoy her and she wished she hadn't bothered to bring it. She usually stuffed her bank card, money and phone in a pocket, but today she felt as though she needed a bag.

She'd also redone her ponytail before she'd left the house, and had changed out of her wellies and into a pair of trainers. She'd even swapped her jodhpurs for a pair of jeans.

Petra had drawn the line at applying a coat of lipstick though, despite picking it up and staring at it. She'd had the silly idea that a bit of colour on her lips might brighten her face, then she'd decided against it. She'd only do what she always did and lick it off before she'd got to where she was going.

Today she was going into the village. They were out of some essentials such as bread and potatoes, and she also wanted to pop into the deli for some of their artisan rose jam and organic cheese. She wanted to take a book to the nursing home, too. There was a little library there, just a couple of shelves, and although Petra didn't have a great deal of time in which to read, she enjoyed a good book, and when she finished with it she took it to the nursing home for others to enjoy.

Picklewick wasn't very large and most people knew everyone else, so as she made her way down the main street she constantly nodded and said hello, and had a couple of quick conversations along the lines of "how are you", "how is Amos" and so on; it was all rather pleasant and a change from the peace of the stables – if you ignored the various horsey noises, the chickens, Princess's frequent bleating, farm machinery...

It had been a while since she'd done anything more than dash into a shop, grab what she wanted and dash back out again, so she took her time in the deli, choosing with care, picking out things she knew Amos would enjoy such as the caramelised onion and walnut chutney to go with the slice of game pie she also bought for him.

'Morning, Petra. We don't see you in the village very often,' a man's voice said from behind and Petra turned to see William Reid, who managed the care home, standing at her elbow waiting to be served.

'Hello, William, how are you? Oh, I've got a book for you.' She drew the paperback out of her bag, wishing she had more than the one to donate.

He took it from her and read the back. 'Thanks, this will be very welcome. There are several residents who get through a book every couple of days and it's hard to keep up with demand.'

'I must pop in for a visit,' she said, feeling guilty. Some of the elderly people in the home had very few relatives who visited them. 'How about if I bring Queenie? Would that be okay?' She knew many of them loved animals, dogs and cats especially, but no longer got a chance to pet any.

'What a lovely idea,' William said, and they made arrangements for her to drop in next week.

Feeling more contented with life than she'd done in a while, she paid for her goodies and strolled further along the street, glancing into shop windows as she went. Faith and Charity's birthday was coming up and she needed to buy something nice for them. Maybe something girly and personal, rather than the horse-related presents she normally gave them. The problem was, she didn't do girly and had little idea what they might like.

Hoping inspiration would strike, she continued along the street. Easter displays were in evidence in shop windows, and dotted along the pavements were large wooden flower beds bursting with spring blooms. Petra loved this time of year, when winter was finally over and the horses and ponies could gorge themselves on the new spring grass (all except poor Tango), and she smiled happily.

Abruptly, her smile disappeared when she saw who was sitting in the window of the café she was walking past, as if they were on display themselves – Harry and Cher, all cosied up and having an intimate discussion by the looks of things.

Petra bit her lip and glanced away. That was that; Harry was more into Cher than Petra had hoped. She'd been right to keep him at arm's length, and she vowed she'd try to keep him out of her thoughts too.

Unfortunately, she had the feeling such a vow might be easier made than kept.

'Timothy?' Harry had arrived home and had just spread out all the paperwork, invoices and receipts he needed to wade through in order to bring his accounts up to date, when his brother phoned. 'Is everything all right?'

'Why shouldn't it be?'

Why, indeed? Harry was so used to being the adult in their little family of two, that he was finding it hard to let go. Timothy was a grown man; he could cope on his own. Part of Harry's reason for moving to Picklewick was to allow him to do just that.

'I can ring my big brother for a chat, can't I?' Timothy added.

'Of course you can, but are you sure you're okay?'

'I'm sure. I'm more concerned about you. I haven't heard from you for a few days.'

Harry blanched. Crikey, Tim was right. The first week he'd arrived in the village he had phoned his brother every day (sometimes twice a day) anxious to ensure he was managing without him. Then Harry had deliberately eased off to every other day.

But it came as a shock to realise he hadn't spoken to Timothy in four days.

'I've, erm, been a little distracted,' he said.

'About time!' his brother exclaimed.

'Eh?'

'What's her name?'

'Whose name?'

'The woman you've been distracted by.'

'I've not been distracted by any woman.'

'Oh, sorry, bro, I just thought...' Harry heard Timothy's sigh. 'What's the distraction, if it's not a girlfriend?'

'Work.'

Timothy snorted. 'You know what they say about all work and no play.'

'Ha ha, very funny.'

'I'm serious, Hal. New job, new home, new woman. Actually, any woman, because I can't remember the last time I saw you with a girl.'

'I've been somewhat busy, if you hadn't noticed.'

'Yeah, sorry about that.'

Harry spluttered, 'You've got nothing to be sorry about.'

'If it weren't for me, you'd—'

'Stop it! I love you, you're my brother. No regrets. Anyway,' Harry took a deep breath and threw the next sentence out there, hoping to alleviate some of the guilt Timothy felt at Harry having to give up his place at university and come home to look after his little brother. It had been a dark time. Harry wasn't entirely sure they'd emerged into the light yet. 'There is someone I'm interested in, if you must know,' he said.

'I knew it!' Timothy crowed. 'What's her name, how did you meet her, is she fit?'

'Slow down. Her name is Petra Kelly and she owns the stables on Muddypuddle

Lane. She's got over twenty animals and—'

'Trust you! I want to know about **her**, not her horses.'

Harry heard Tim's exasperated laugh. 'She's um, early thirties I think, slim, fairly tall, blond hair, green eyes. No, they're blue. No, green – they're green. And she's got a couple of freckles on her nose.'

'She sounds cute.'

'She is.'

'Harry?'

'Yes?'

'You really need to get close enough to check out her eye colour, man.'

'Green-blue,' he said, decisively.

'Are you sure you're not making her up, like an imaginary friend?'

'I'm not making her up. I'm not sure if she's a friend, though. I don't think she likes me much.'

'How can she not like you? You're the best guy I know.'

'You're biased.'

'And you need to turn on the charm and try harder.'

'Thanks for the advice,' Harry replied in a dry voice. But maybe his baby brother was right. Harry had taken his cue from Petra, but perhaps he should be a bit more forthright. She might not realise he was interested in her.

On the other hand, she might not want him to be interested in her and any advances on his part might be unwelcome. And if that were the case, she might decide his services as a farrier were unwelcome too, and he'd be in danger of losing an important client, a client who hadn't been all that convinced of him in the first place.

His instinct was right; it was best if he carried on behaving the same way towards her, and hope he'd recognise the signs if she did want anything more than a professional relationship.

As far as Harry was concerned, the ball was very firmly in Petra's court.

CHAPTER SEVEN

Petra had just shoved a large forkful of pasta in her mouth when the landline rang. With a garbled curse and frantically chewing, she went to answer it. Clients rang at all times of the day and night, and although she wished they'd stick to reasonable hours – to be fair, it was only seven p.m. so this call wasn't totally unreasonable and some evenings she'd still be in the arena at this time teaching a lesson – she didn't want to miss a potential booking. Or a cancellation.

Hoping it wasn't the latter, she swallowed her mouthful and picked up the phone.

Her heart did a funny little skipped beat when she heard the voice on the other end.

'Hi Petra, it's Harry.'

'What do you want?' She knew she was being rude, but she couldn't help it. Besides, it was usually her who called the farrier, not the other way around.

There was a slight hesitation then he said, 'I was checking that we're still on for tomorrow.'

Eh? Still on for what? As she was racking her brains, he spoke again.

'I've got Ted's diary in front of me and he has put the stables down for a possible re-shoe of nine animals.'

'Ah, yes, I see.'

'Do you still want me to come?'

'I suppose. Ted never used to ring – he just turned up.'

'I like to double-check. There's no point in a wasted journey.'

Petra did a rapid run-through of the condition of her charges' hooves. Although she checked each horse and pony thoroughly every day, she couldn't for the life of her remember who needed re-shoeing. She always left that to Ted, trusting implicitly that he wouldn't re-shoe an animal when it didn't need it.

'You'd better come. What time have you got me down for?'

'Early. Eight o'clock.'

'I'll see you then,' she said and hung up before he could say anything further.

As she returned to the table, she noticed Amos was frowning at her. 'What?' she asked, sliding back into her seat and picking up her cutlery.

'I take it that was the new farrier on the phone?'

Petra nodded, her attention on her meal. For some reason, her appetite had deserted her.

'Why were you so abrupt with him?' Amos asked.

She moved her pasta around in the bowl and didn't answer.

'What has he done to upset you?' her uncle persisted, and she could feel his eyes on her. 'I know you can be a bit grumpy—'

'I am not grumpy,' she interrupted grumpily.

'Cranky, then?'

'No! And cranky means the same thing as grumpy. I prefer the word "succinct".'

'I prefer the word "cross" and "rude",' Amos retorted.

'That's two words.'

'They both fit.'

'They do not!'

'You know they do, but you're not usually this bad.'

Petra placed her knife and fork neatly together in the bowl. 'If you must know, I'm not too keen on the company he keeps.'

'Oh? Pray tell.'

'Cher Reynolds. They're an item, and I'm surprised, that's all.'

'What do you mean? I thought he was single.'

'I saw them together. They looked very cosy in the café in the village.'

Amos frowned again, his already craggy brow creasing even further. 'I'm sure there's nothing going on between them.'

'It certainly looked as if there was, to me.' Petra knew what she saw – a lunchtime date. Cher hadn't been able to keep her hands off him.

'I heard on the grapevine that Cher is thinking of buying Thaila her own pony. Or rather, her ex-husband is,' Amos said.

Petra's eyes widened. 'I hope she doesn't think she's going to stable it here.'

He chuckled. 'I doubt it. There's no love lost between you two, is there? Anyway, I don't think she's going to bother after all. I heard that she was all for the idea and had asked Harry to accompany her, but she seems to have gone off the boil when he said no.'

'Hmph, they looked friendly enough to me when I saw them.'

'Looks can be deceiving. I heard he didn't even stay to finish his drink.'

'You hear an awful lot,' she accused, wondering where he was getting his information from.

'That's because I go out and talk to people. Which reminds me, you couldn't drive me to the Black Horse later, could you? It's darts and a chippie supper tonight.'

'You've just had your evening meal,' she protested.

'Aye, but I'm not going to turn down a pint and a plate of chips in the pub.'

As Petra cleared away the dishes (Amos had emptied his bowl – she'd hardly touched hers), she thought about what her uncle had told her. She could have sworn Harry and Cher were a couple, or at least on the brink of becoming one, but maybe she'd got it wrong. Admittedly, she wasn't as good at reading people as she was at reading horses. Her animals mightn't be able to speak, but she was able to tell what they were feeling much better than she was able to tell what was in people's minds.

Hell, she was having trouble knowing what was in her own, because for some reason the news that Harry was single and wasn't interested in Cher had lifted her spirits immensely.

And she knew she was in trouble when she found herself humming along to the radio after she'd dropped Amos off at the pub.

She knew she was in **serious** trouble when she took the long way home – past the cottage Harry was renting.

Lights were on behind drawn curtains, and her treacherous mind couldn't help wondering whether he was thinking about her as much as she was thinking about him.

Harry wasn't pleased. His perfectly polite and reasonable phone call to Petra had left him feeling cross and deflated, and he failed to understand what was wrong with the woman. He'd been nothing but friendly to her, his conduct utterly professional, but she'd been rude and rather dismissive in return. He was beginning to think that Cher had a point.

A low-level feeling of dread crept over him; he wasn't looking forward to visiting the stables on Muddypuddle Lane tomorrow, and he debated whether or not to cancel the appointment. But that would mean calling Petra back, and he seriously didn't fancy speaking to her again this evening. She'd spoilt his mood enough already. Then there were the horses to consider; they could last another week or two without being seen by a farrier, and although Harry wasn't under the illusion that he was the only one for miles around (he wasn't – farriers were quite common, especially in rural areas), they did tend to be booked up.

Taking a deep breath, he resolved to attend the stables tomorrow, and whilst he was there he'd have it out with her. He didn't want to lose her custom, but neither could he work for someone who clearly disliked him so much. Ted had given him the impression that she was offish with most people, but the way she was with him took being offish to the extreme. He was used to surly trainers, brusque farmers, and the like, but she took the biscuit.

Harry paused. Or, did she? When he thought about it, she had behaved no differently to that of a number of other horsey people he'd encountered, so why did her attitude towards him bother him so much?

It was because he fancied her, he decided, and he'd taken it as a personal affront. If she'd been a bloke would he have reacted the same way? Probably not. Therefore the problem lay with him and not her. Petra was, as far as he could tell, simply being Petra. He needed to grow a thicker skin and get over himself.

Vowing not to take it personally and deciding he wouldn't take her to task about it after all, he nevertheless spent the rest of the evening trying to keep thoughts of Petra out of his head.

Hope for the best and plan for the worst; Harry couldn't remember where he'd heard such sage advice, but the following morning he drove the old van up the bumpy track to Petra's stables, filled with optimism that she would be pleasant (or should he say, pleasanter) but fully expecting his visit to be as disagreeable as the last time he'd met her.

Several curious faces peered out of the horseboxes, ears pricked, following his progress across the yard to his usual parking spot.

Horses were intelligent creatures and he had no doubt that they recognised Ted's van and knew what it signified.

He cut the engine and clambered out, stretching his back and rotating his shoulders. Blacksmithing was a physical job and he hadn't rested too well last night (Petra had featured quite heavily in his dreams, but he couldn't for the life of him remember any of them this morning) and he was feeling rather tired and in no mood for her unfriendly attitude, despite his vow yesterday evening to not take it personally.

'Morning.' Petra appeared from around a corner and smiled at him.

Harry nearly lost his balance. 'Morning,' he replied cautiously, wondering why she was smiling.

'Nice day.'

It certainly was, bright, sunny, and fresh, yet with a hint of warmth from the spring sun. 'Yes, it's lovely,' he agreed. 'Are they all here?' He gestured towards the animals in their stalls.

'Yep, all there. Most of them are okay with being shod, except for Gerald. He doesn't have shoes, but he will need to have his hooves trimmed.'

'Remind me, which one is Gerald?'

Petra pointed to an empty stall.

Harry squinted then he laughed. He could just about see a pair of incredibly long equine ears waggling over the top of the half-door and realised they belonged to the donkey.

'He came to us in a dreadful state,' Petra was saying. 'I was only supposed to have him for a couple of weeks while he got his strength back, but I ended up keeping him.'

'That was good of you.'

She shrugged. 'He earns his keep at Christmas,' she said. 'Nativity plays and so on.'

Harry wasn't fooled. He understood that, as far as Petra was concerned, Gerald earning his keep didn't matter one iota to her, and despite the barriers she put up to keep people at bay, she had a heart of gold when it came to animals. He suspected she might also have one when

it came to people who needed help too,
but he couldn't prove it.

She didn't wait for a response from him,
but went to the nearest stall and led out
a small creamy-coloured cob. 'This is
Parsnip. Named for the colour of his coat
and for the way he digs his heels into the
ground when he doesn't want to do
something.'

Harry smiled at the metaphor – parsnips
had long taproots and were sometimes
difficult to dig up. The pony was a
beautiful colour though, especially with
the early morning sun shining on him. It
gave his coat a soft gold sheen. He was
about to say so, when he glanced from
the pony to the woman who was holding
him, and the sight stopped his breath.

The same sun shone on Petra's hair, and
he was reminded of those religious

paintings where the subject had a halo around their heads. Some of her hair had escaped from its customary bun and her face was framed in shades of gold and bronze. Her face was also illuminated by the rays and her skin appeared luminous, her eyes bluer than he remembered; he could have sworn they had more green in them—

'Is everything all right?' she asked, bringing him back to himself with a start.

'Oh, yes, fine. Great. Never better.' He was stammering and stuttering like an idiot, but he didn't seem able to get his brain to work, and what was coming out of his mouth was nonsensical drivel.

'Good.' She shot him a curious look, but he turned his attention back to Parsnip.

'Right, I'll get started on these. Is there anything else I should know about?' he asked.

'Nothing, except Blaze – he's the chestnut without a blaze – doesn't like his hind feet being played with, so if you can get away with not shoeing him today, it would be good.'

'Blaze **without** a blaze?'

Petra smiled at him again and his heart somersaulted. God, she was incredibly pretty when she smiled. She was pretty anyway, but her face lit up like a Madonna when she did that. A beautiful Madonna—

'Are you sure you're okay?' she asked. 'You look a bit strange.'

'Do you fancy going out for a drink sometime? Or a meal?' He stopped abruptly, appalled at what he'd just asked her.

She sent him another odd look. It seemed like odd looks and smiles were the order of the day. 'You don't look as though you want me to go anywhere with you,' she pointed out and he hurriedly rearranged his expression.

'Oh, I do, believe me, I really do,' he insisted.

'In that case, yes. Just the once, mind you; don't think I'm going to be making a habit of it.'

He didn't care that she was only planning on going out with him once. It was a far cry from not going out with him at all.

And you never know, he said to himself, once might very well lead to twice.

'Brilliant!' He beamed back at her. 'Tonight?' He held the grin in place, but at the same time he was berating himself for sounding so keen. Or desperate, which was possibly more accurate.

'I can do eight. I've got lessons booked until seven-thirty.'

'Is eight going to give you enough time to get ready?' From past experiences (not that there had been a great many of them) he was under the impression that women could take hours to get ready to go out.

Petra gave him an incredulous look. 'I don't need long,' she replied frostily, 'unless you think it's going to take hours to get this,' she swept a hand from her head to her knees, 'to look presentable.'

'I...no...that's not what I meant,' he stammered. 'You can come as you are, I don't mind.'

This time she looked more amused than affronted. 'Covered in horse hair and smelling of manure?'

'I didn't mean that either. What I mean is, you're beautiful anyway and a posh dress or lipstick won't make you any more beautiful than you already are.'

Petra studied him for a long while, then she said in a small voice, 'That's the nicest thing anyone has ever said to me.' And with that she shoved Parsnip's lead rein into his hands and was off, almost running across the yard.

Harry watched her go, so many emotions tumbling through his chest that he didn't know where to start in sorting them out.

But when she stopped as she reached the corner of the stable block and turned to him, he saw the delight on her face, and then his overriding emotion was pleasure. He'd made her happy, and as a consequence, it made him happy too.

In fact, he was happier today than he could ever remember being, and all that had happened was that he'd asked her out and she'd said yes.

Lord help him, he was smitten. And it felt good.

That was unexpected, Petra thought for the umpteenth time that day, as she hurried to get ready for her date with Harry. The twins were happy to see to the three ponies which had been used for the lesson that had just finished, although they did keep shooting her curious glances and whispering between themselves.

They thought she hadn't noticed, but she had, and their odd behaviour set her teeth on edge. So what if she was having a quick drink with a man this evening? It wasn't the first time – although, she was forced to acknowledge, it was probably such a rare event everyone had forgotten about it. In fact, she was struggling to remember when the last time was and who it had been with.

Despite telling Harry that she didn't spend hours getting ready, Petra had spent hours mentally going through her wardrobe and wondering what she should wear. At least her hair had been freshly washed that morning, so all she needed to do was to release it from its band and give it a quick brush after the fastest shower in the history of mankind; she was well aware that l'eau de horse wasn't to everyone's taste, and even though Harry might work with horses himself, he probably didn't want his date smelling of one.

That **was** what this was, wasn't it – a date?

She'd assumed so, but what if she was wrong? Had she read too much into what might have been a casual suggestion, and this was nothing more than a swift half down the pub?

Now look what she'd gone and done; she was second-guessing and overanalysing.

Just turn up and see what happens, she told herself. As long as she didn't make a fool of herself and she let him make the first move (if, indeed, any first moves were going to be made), then all would be well.

But as she drove into the village, which was thankfully only five minutes away by car, she was seriously wondering why she'd agreed to have a drink with him at all. She didn't normally go out at night. For one thing she was often too tired, for another she couldn't be bothered because there was nowhere to go in Picklewick except for the Black Horse, and for a third, no one asked her.

Petra was sorely tempted to turn her SUV around and send Harry a text to say something had come up.

But she was here now, she argued to herself, as she drew to a stop in the pub's car park. Just one drink wouldn't hurt and perhaps a quick bite to eat because she hadn't had any supper yet and she was starving.

She glanced down, checking that she looked decent enough in her jeans, smart leather pumps and flowery top (the effect was somewhat spoilt by the old and worn waxed-cotton jacket she'd slung over the top because it was decidedly chilly this evening) and came to the conclusion that she'd do. This was as close to dressing up as she got. He'd have to take her or leave her.

From the look in his eyes when he caught sight of her from his table near the bar, she guessed he must like what he saw. He did a sort of double-take, swiftly scanned her from head to foot, then his gaze came to rest on her face, and she was certain there was admiration in it. There was a hint of something else too, but she wasn't sure what.

He got to his feet as she approached and held out both hands to her.

Cautiously, she took hold of them and he pulled her gently towards him, kissing the air near to one side of her face then the other.

With a sharp intake of breath, she pulled her hand free and stepped back.

For a second there, she'd thought he was about to go in for a proper kiss, and while she would have pushed him away, a little part of her was disappointed that it was only a peck on the cheek.

Mystified, she sat down. Harry remained standing.

'What can I get you?' he asked.

'Erm, soda and lime, please.' Petra watched him walk to the bar, taking in his long legs encased in dark denim, his broad shoulders beneath a plain white tee shirt, the set of his back, the shape of his behind.

Oh my, this wouldn't do at all.

Not only had his extremely friendly greeting disconcerted her, now she was ogling his backside. Having never been much of a hugger (not when it came to people), she wasn't used to such familiarity, and although she was fully aware that many people greeted each other like that, it wasn't her way, and now her heart was thudding and she had butterflies in her tummy. Surely a simple 'hello' and a nod would have sufficed?

Or maybe this was a proper date, and that's how datees usually greeted each other these days?

Harry returned with their drinks and a couple of menus. 'I don't know about you,' he said, 'but I'm starving. I didn't have a chance to grab anything to eat before I came out; I got stuck over Willow Hill way, working with a vet to treat a lame gelding.

'Oh?' Petra was interested – anything horsey was of interest to her and at least she was in her comfort zone when she was talking about equines. She might learn something too, so as they chose their meals and waited for their food to arrive, Harry explained that the horse in question had severe laminitis.

Petra shuddered. Laminitis, she knew, could be very serious and she thought about Tango and how he made her feel terribly guilty about putting his grazing muzzle on him. 'One of mine is prone to laminitis,' she said.

'The bright chestnut one?'

Petra smiled. 'Tango – yes, he is rather bright, isn't he? It makes him easy to spot. He's a sweetie but he hates having his muzzle on.'

'I bet he does,' Harry said, leaning to one side as a plate of steak and chips was placed in front of him. 'Imagine being given a meal like this and being told you had to eat it through a straw, which is what I imagine trying to graze on all that new grass whilst wearing his muzzle must feel like to him.'

Petra laughed. 'That would be awful.' She eyed her food with appreciation. 'Mmm, this looks good.'

'Do you often miss your evening meal?' he asked, spearing a chip.

'Only when I'm asked to go to the pub.'

His expression was neutral. 'Does that happen much?'

'Never.' She may as well be honest with him. 'I haven't been on a date in years.' As soon as the words passed her lips she immediately wanted to take them back. If this wasn't a date, then she'd just made a right fool of herself.

'Neither have I,' Harry said, and Petra blinked in surprise.

'A good-looking man like you? I'm shocked.' She really needed to give her mouth a stern talking to, because it was saying things her brain hadn't given it permission to say. What was wrong with her this evening? She was behaving like a gauche schoolgirl. Although, saying that, the schoolgirls who frequented her stables were far from gauche – they were self-assured, precocious and confident. The total opposite of Petra, and she was double their age.

A smile spread across his face. 'You think I'm good-looking?'

She gulped and examined her plate, wishing the ground would open up and swallow her. Now, please.

'I think you're beautiful,' he said.

She risked a quick glance at him. He didn't look as though he was joking.

'I mean it,' he added. 'You're lovely.'

'Thank you,' she whispered. Unused to compliments, she was unsure how to deal with this.

'Thank you, for agreeing to come out with me this evening,' he countered. 'I didn't think you would. I didn't think you liked me.'

Her gaze shot to his face once more. 'I didn't.'

'But you do now?' He looked like a hopeful puppy begging for food.

She nodded.

'Good, because I like you, too. Now we've got that out of the way, shall we continue with our meal?'

Thankful for the distraction of her supper, Petra tucked in, and while they ate they chatted once more about horses until she felt at ease again.

'Have you always worked with horses?' she asked him.

'Yes, my mother loved to ride, and I learnt to ride before I could walk, so I grew up around them.'

'Does she still ride?' Riding, unlike many other sports, could be carried on until well into middle-age and beyond.

'My parents died when I was twenty. Car crash.'

Petra's heart ached for him. 'I'm so very sorry,' she said, wanting to reach out but not knowing where to start.

'It was a long time ago,' he said, but she could hear the anguish behind his words and see the sadness in his face.

'Did you ever want to be a professional rider or trainer?' She knew she was changing the subject but his sorrow made her want to weep for him.

'I thought about it but my brother took up most of my time.'

'You've got a brother? I wish I had a sibling or two. What's his name? How old is he? Where does he live?'

'He's called Timothy, he's twenty-four, nearly twenty-five and he's still living in the family home near Cheltenham.'

Petra did the maths. 'That meant he was quite young when...?' She trailed off,

dismay and pity flooding through her.
'That must have been tough.'

His smile was small. 'It was. I was at uni
when I got the call. I jacked in the course
to look after him.'

'You must have been devastated.'

He shrugged. 'We were, but we had no
choice other than to get on with it. I
didn't want Tim to go to my aunt and
uncle, although they did want him to. He
insisted on staying in the house he'd
always known as home. I stayed to look
after him, and fell in with a local farrier
who offered to train me. He knew my
mum and what had happened to our
parents, and was kind enough to let me
work for him and fit my hours around
Tim's school holidays. He sometimes used
to let me bring Tim with me, and Tim
loved it. Not the farrier side of things, but

the horses. He'd learnt to ride when he was tiny, too.'

'What does he do now?'

'He's a vet,' Harry said proudly. 'He's working for a practice which specialises in equine health back in Cheltenham. It's only a locum position, but at least he's earning a wage and it's good experience for him.'

'What were you studying at university?' she asked, but she had a sinking feeling she knew the answer.

'Veterinary Science.'

He'd confirmed her suspicion. 'Now that your brother is fledged, so to speak, do you think you'll go back to it?' she asked.

Harry laughed. 'Not a chance! I've seen how hard Timothy works and I don't fancy the unsociable hours, either. I'm happy doing what I'm doing, thanks.'

'That's good.' She meant it. It would be awful if he was regretting not being a vet, and he did have a point about the unsociable hours. As a farrier, he might get the odd call-out on the weekend, but they would be few and far between. She worked worse hours than he did, because her busiest times tended to be weekends and evenings. Vets, though, were often on-call throughout the night and on weekends.

'What about you?' he asked her. 'Amos is your uncle, isn't he?'

Petra nodded. 'I've been horse-mad ever since I can remember. My parents live in Norwich but we used to come and visit Uncle Amos and Aunty Mags a couple of times every year, and I used to howl fit to burst when they took me home. I wanted to stay so badly that they eventually gave in when I was about eighteen and let me move in with Amos. Aunt Mags had passed on by then, so I think they thought I might be company for him. Little did they know that I'd be here and still loving it twelve years later.'

There was a small pause in the conversation, then Harry said, 'I take it there's no significant other in your life right now?'

She gave him a level look. 'I wouldn't have agreed to have a drink with you if there was.'

'Fair enough, I had to check.'

'How about you?'

Harry grinned and said, 'I wouldn't have asked you to have a drink with me if there was.'

Petra raised her almost empty glass and tipped it towards him. 'Fair enough,' she echoed back at him.

'Do you fancy a proper drink?' he asked.

'I'd love one, but I'm driving.'

'I can walk you home, if you like. It's not that far and the exercise will do me good,' he offered.

'Just the one, then.'

He bought her a pint of ale and one for himself, and they drank and chatted until it started to get late.

Petra was amazed at how quickly the evening passed, and to her surprise she found she didn't want it to end. She was enjoying herself immensely.

After the initial horsey-talk, the conversation moved on from families and onto things that had nothing at all to do with equines or stables, blacksmithing or businesses. They discussed the cinema and books, the news, favourite places, favourite food.

'What's your favourite time of the year?' he asked.

'Spring.'

'Mine, too. I think it's the promise of summer.'

'What's your favourite time of the day?' she asked. It was a silly, frivolous game, but Harry seemed to be enjoying it as much as she.

'Early morning,' he replied.

'And mine! Everything is so fresh and new.'

'I used to like early mornings because Timothy was asleep and not playing loud music, or stomping around the house,' Harry explained. 'Of course, it's different now I'm living on my own. If loud music is playing, I only have myself to blame.' He looked at his watch.

Petra checked the time on her phone.

They arrived at the same conclusion at the same time – it was getting late and both of them had to get up early.

Not caring if she looked a mess in it, Petra slipped her old jacket on and did the zip up. Harry was wearing the sort of jacket hikers favoured, so both of them should have been warm enough as they walked along Muddypuddle Lane. But for some reason Petra shivered and no sooner had she done so, than his arm came around her shoulders and he pulled her into him.

'Is that better?' he asked and she nodded, her cheek rubbing against his shoulder.

He smelt divine, citrus with a hit of wood, and she breathed deeply, drawing the scent of him into her and savouring it. It was also nice being held by him, his chest warm against her side, his solid arm curled around her.

She didn't want him to release her but of course he had to, giving her another one of those double-kisses as he did so.

'I enjoyed myself this evening,' he said.

'So did I.'

'Does that mean you'll come out with me again?'

'Yes.'

'When?'

'I'll have to check my diary,' she said, then hastily added, 'I really will have to check it – I can't remember what's booked in.'

'Okay. You've got my number.' He hesitated, and she wondered if he was about to kiss her.

When he didn't, disappointment flowed through her.

She was still disappointed when she fell asleep a short while later. But at least he'd said he wanted to see her again, so she had to be content with that for the time being.

CHAPTER EIGHT

Harry lifted the horse's hind leg so that the animal's hoof rested in the foot stand, and unrolled his bag of tools. He had to remove the old shoe, then trim the hoof in preparation for the new one. The horse he was working on was familiar with the process and stood patiently munching on a hay net and totally ignoring the human messing with his feet.

Harry wished he was as calm as the horse.

His head was full of Petra and nothing he did and no matter how busy he was, could drive her image from his mind. That she'd agreed to see him again made his stomach knot with anticipation and his heart thud.

The impulse that had made him ask her out had been a good one, despite how he'd felt about it at the time. He'd enjoyed himself last night, and he was delighted with the way the date had gone, although he had been worried that she hadn't considered it a date. But she had, and he was so pleased with himself, he was like a dog with two tails.

Petra, he'd discovered, was good company and they had more in common than he would ever have guessed – aside from the equine connection, of course. Once you got to know her she wasn't in the least bit grumpy, but he realised that she didn't suffer fools gladly and tended to prefer animals to people. He could relate to that. He'd had to be gregarious because of Timothy and also because of his job, to a certain extent. He might deal with surly owners on a regular basis, but owners, surly or otherwise, didn't appreciate a surly farrier. Ted had been an exception; he'd built up a good reputation and people had become used to him. Harry was in a new area with new clients – he couldn't afford to cheese any of them off. That didn't mean that when it came to certain people (he was thinking of Cher Reynolds) then a pony was definitely preferable. Being his own boss suited him and for the most part he was usually left alone to get on with the job of shoeing.

If he had a choice he tended to gravitate away from people, so he and Petra were more alike than he'd thought. He simply hid it better. Although one person he would like to gravitate towards was Petra herself.

Harry shook his head in annoyance. He needed to concentrate on what he was doing. The horse he was shoeing was unconcerned but no matter how gentle the animal, horses were flighty and unpredictable. Letting your guard down and day dreaming wasn't advisable. But no matter how hard he tried to concentrate, Petra's sweet face or something she'd said popped into his head, and he found he couldn't wait to see her again.

As soon as he'd loaded his tools and assorted equipment into the van, Harry was unable to resist the urge any longer — he had to phone her. He might not be able to see her right now, but he could hear her voice and if he knew when their next date was he might be able to relax.

His stomach clenched when she answered, and he wondered where she was and what she was doing right now. He wanted to ask, but was worried he might come across as a bit stalkerish, so instead he said, 'How are you fixed for later? Have you got any lessons?' She was almost certain to be busy, but he had to ask.

'Gosh, you're keen.'

Yes, he was. He couldn't deny it, and he hesitated, wondering how to respond.

'I was planning on taking Hercules out for a ride,' she continued, ignoring his embarrassed silence. 'He's not been ridden for ages and he gets bored easily. I caught him nibbling the lower part of his door this morning. If he's not careful he's going to be pooping wood.'

'I could come with you?' he suggested, suddenly.

The phone went silent and Harry hoped he hadn't overstepped the mark or misconstrued their connection last night.

Eventually, she said quietly, 'I'd like that,' then she added, 'Be at the stables at four-thirty.'

Harry couldn't wait!

The clang as an iron shoe struck a stone provided a backdrop to the rhythmic percussion thud of hooves on earth, and Petra relaxed in the saddle as the familiar music soothed her. Riding out on the open moors above the valley was her happy place. For her, nothing could beat being on horseback on a surprisingly warm spring afternoon, surrounded by nature, and with no sign of people apart from the steady drone of a tractor in the distance and a line of fencing disappearing over the brow of a hill.

Oh, and the man at her side.

She was extremely aware of him, all right, especially the way his body gently swayed with the horse's gait, the curl of hair poking out from underneath his helmet, his strong forearms with their rolled-up sleeves, one of them resting loosely on his thighs. Those thighs didn't escape her notice, either. Clad in black jodhpurs, they were muscular and she was more aware of them than she could ever remember being of anyone else's legs.

His thighs weren't the only part of him she was aware of. Every so often his citrussy scent laced with woody undertones and another delicious smell she could only assume was his own unique scent, would waft across her nose. Together with the aroma of horse, leather tack and the great outdoors, she thought she might be becoming slightly intoxicated. She felt a little lightheaded and it wasn't an unpleasant feeling at all.

Then there was his profile, and she also caught glimpses of the rest of his face as he gazed at the countryside unfolding around them. Now and again their eyes would meet, and Petra would swiftly look away, but not before she saw the smile he gave her.

Petra was used to having other people with her when she rode because she was frequently supervising a group of riders who liked to hack, and this didn't bother her because riding was riding no matter who accompanied her – and riding was better than anything else in the world.

But her absolute favourite thing to do was to ride solo. She loved her alone time with her horse and her dog, who was busily sniffing every blade of grass and every rock; Queenie's tail was wagging so hard it was little more than a blur. Being alone gave her the opportunity to recharge her batteries, and she guarded it jealously.

But when Harry suggested he came with her on her ride, she was intrigued. She wanted to see how well he rode for a start – and she also wanted to see what it would be like to have him by her side.

It wasn't a date, more of a trial run for being in a relationship, because she'd never felt like this about any man. She had never given anyone else the opportunity to get close to her, and she was scared by her feelings and worried at how he'd fit into her life – if, in fact, things got that far. She reasoned that it was better to know now rather than to wait until she was even more invested in their growing relationship to find out.

Then there was also the issue of what if she fell in love (although she feared she might be half-way there already) – what was she supposed to do about it? Was there any room in her busy life for love?

Pushing the unsettling thoughts away, Petra tried to concentrate on the new buds on the branches of the trees and shrubs dotting the path. Some of the leaves had already unfurled and the array of green made her spirits soar, as did the complicated song of a blackbird perched on the very highest top of a nearby tree. His bright yellow beak contrasted sharply with his black plumage and she wished him all the luck in the world in his quest for a mate.

The bird's sweet song followed them as they rode higher, soon leaving the neatly fenced fields behind as they negotiated a gate which led onto the hillside above.

Petra breathed deeply, the fresh air invigorating her and making her feel more alive than she had in a long time. Although she forced herself to acknowledge that it may well be partly due to Harry's aftershave, and she longed to get close enough to him to bury her nose in his neck.

Unable to bear her jumbled thoughts any longer, Petra urged Hercules into a canter, then before she knew it the pair of them were galloping wildly along the dirt track, the horse's mane snapping, the wind buffeting her face, her heart pounding with the sheer unbridled joy of a horse and rider at one with nature.

She whooped in exhilaration, letting Hercules have his head, trusting him to take care on the path, and allowing him to run at his own pace. She was dimly aware of Queenie racing alongside, bounding through the tufts of grass, a black shadow with a pink lolling tongue and flapping ears.

She was also aware of Harry keeping pace with her, Midnight's nose almost touching Hercules's flank. When she risked a quick look over her shoulder she saw that he was up in his stirrups and crouching over the horse's neck, trying to keep wind drag to a minimum, and she laughed. He'd need all the help he could get if he wanted to keep up with her; Midnight was no match for Hercules.

Desperate to leave him eating her dust, she urged her mount on with a shout and a slap of the reins on his neck. Hercules, though, had other ideas, and he gradually slowed.

Harry pulled on Midnight's reins and his horse slowed in tandem, ensuring he stayed a few paces behind her.

Was Midnight as blown as Hercules, or was Harry being a gentleman and allowing her to "win", even though they hadn't officially been racing and there was no finishing post as such, although she had been heading for a stand of trees which she knew signified the start of a small valley with a tumbling brook running through it.

As her horse came to a walk, his sides heaving and blowing hard, another idea came to her – maybe Harry had been staying slightly behind her just in case she fell off (she wanted to scoff at that, but she had been known to come a cropper now and again), and the thought warmed her immeasurably. Most other riders would have done their best to win, especially with Hercules flagging – bless him, he was getting on a bit and he wasn't as fit as he had once been. Still, she could tell he'd enjoyed himself, because he kept tossing his head with his neck arched and he even managed a little prance for a step or two.

Petra watched Harry out of the corner of her eye as he drew level, Midnight just as winded as Hercules, and once again she saw his easy grace in the saddle and his confidence in his ability to work with his horse – because it was partnership, not dominance, that made her own relationship with Hercules so special.

Calling Queenie to heel (or as near to the back end of a horse as the dog felt comfortable getting) Petra guided Hercules into the trees, the ground dropping away and forcing her to lean back in the saddle to counterbalance her weight with the gradient. She allowed the horse to pick his way down the path, confident that he knew where he was going.

And as she rode, Amos's advice about not leaving it too late rang in her ears.

So when they reached the little clearing, the brook widening into a small pool, she brought her horse to a halt.

It was now or never, she said to herself, sliding from the saddle, her heart in her mouth and ponies cavorting in her tummy.

Harry had still been panting a little when Petra had turned Hercules towards a clump of trees and began to head down the hillside, following the woodland which was lining the sides of a narrow valley.

The gallop had been fun – he hadn't ridden like that in ages, and he'd forgotten how exciting it could be. It was also hard work on the body, and he knew he'd feel the effect tomorrow, despite being relatively fit, especially his thighs, shoulders and behind.

The little valley was barely more than a crease in the landscape, yet it was a different world to that of the relatively bare hillside above. Sounds were more intimate with the mottled and gnarled trunks muffling noise, yet the birdsong was clearer, sharper and far more numerous. The little creatures flitted and darted, chattering and chirping as they went, and the spaniel was in her element as she tried unsuccessfully to chase them. Once or twice she came across a squirrel digging amongst the dead leaves, searching for the last of the winter's stored nuts, but they were always too quick for her, bounding for the nearest trunk and leaping up it, leaving Queenie to snuffle and sniff in frantic circles as she tried to work out where it had disappeared to, and Harry chuckling at the dog's antics.

He was so engrossed in Queenie's confusion, that he almost failed to notice that Petra had brought Hercules to a halt. Wondering what she was doing, he watched her lift her leg elegantly over the saddle and slide off the horse's back to land lightly on her feet amongst the fallen leaves.

The stream they'd been following had flowed into a small clearing and had formed a little pool, which was a perfect place to water the horses, so he dismounted too and led Midnight to it.

Both horses slurped noisily, sucking the cool liquid into their mouths with mobile lips. When they'd had their fill, Hercules entertained himself by pawing at the water, sending spray into the air to fall back in sparkling droplets. Midnight had his fun by blowing bubbles and snorting, the fuzzy hairs on his nose and chin soaking wet.

When he attempted to rub his face in Harry's coat, Harry gathered up the reins and prepared to mount up. He was just about to put his foot in the stirrup when he noticed Petra throw Hercules's reins over the nearest bush, and the horse immediately dropped his head and started cropping the tufts of grass which grew along the banks of the stream.

Intrigued, Harry waited for a moment but when it became clear that Petra didn't intend to leave the pretty clearing yet, he took care to tie his horse up after briefly debating whether to do the same as her and hope Midnight didn't realise he wasn't secured to anything. Not wanting to take the chance and certainly not wanting to chase after the gelding as it headed back to the stables, he double-checked the knot before turning around to see what Petra was doing.

She was standing close, her face lifted to the canopy, a dreamy expression in her eyes.

Harry stilled; he'd never seen her look dreamy before and he wondered what she was thinking. She looked gorgeous with the sun shining through the new leaves and dappling her skin and hair with light and shadow. It reminded him of a woodland nymph he'd once seen in a painting – she looked as though she was cloaked in magic and touched by fairy dust as little motes danced around her head.

My god, she was so beautiful it took his breath away.

'I love it here,' she said. 'Not many people come down this way because the path runs out further along.'

'It's beautiful,' he agreed but he was referring to her and not the clearing.

Harry waited for her to say something else but she continued to stand motionless, so he did too, allowing the peace of the place seep into him, hearing nothing but the soft stamp of a hoof, the jingle of tack, and the sounds of nature.

It was so peaceful, he thought he could hear her heart beating. He could most definitely hear his own.

'I come here to refill my soul with all that is good,' she said, breaking the silence.

Harry knew what she meant. 'I've missed this. I've been so busy, so wrapped up in Tim, work and life in general, I think I'd forgotten how to live.'

He stared at her.

Her eyes were luminous, her lips slightly parted, and he knew that if he lived to be a hundred, he'd never forget the sight of her.

Petra's gaze locked onto his and she took a step closer to him.

Then another.

He couldn't tear himself away – her eyes were greener than the gurgling pool, unfathomable depths where a man could easily lose himself and drown.

He might be drowning right now; his chest was tight, the air heavy in his lungs, his thoughts languid. She was bewitching him, bespelling him to fall in love with her like the mystical naiads of ancient Greece, who lived in pools and lakes and were irresistible to men.

Harry didn't want to resist her. He didn't think he could...

Another step brought her close enough for him to gather her into his arms if he wanted.

And he did want, very much. But he instinctively knew that he had to take his cue from her. If he was too eager or made any sudden move, he was terrified she might slip into those mysterious waters and be lost to him forever.

She tilted her chin and her lips parted a little more.

Harry resisted the urge to lick his own in nerves.

The sounds of the brook, the chirping of the birds, the rustle of the leaves overhead as the wind sighed through them, had all faded. The only noise was the pulse in his ears and his heart hammering a staccato beat.

'Then I shall have to remind you how to live,' she murmured, and she stretched up on tiptoe, her arms snaking around his neck as she drew his head down to hers.

And in that wonderful moment when their lips met, Harry forgot everything – except for one thing. He remembered what it was like to be truly alive.

CHAPTER NINE

'Hey, bro, how's it going?' Timothy sounded upbeat and cheerful on the other end of the phone.

'Great. How about you?' Harry was more than great, actually... The kisses he'd shared with Petra floated through his mind, making him smile.

'Eh, you know. Work, eat, sleep, work, Xbox, work...' his brother said. 'What have you been getting up to?'

'I went riding yesterday.'

'With your imaginary friend?'

'How can you possibly know that?'

'Because I know you. You sound different. Happy.'

Harry **was** happy, but he didn't think he'd been unhappy before. 'Gee, thanks.'

'You **do**,' Timothy insisted. 'And I'm happy for you. I take it she's decided she likes you after all?'

'I haven't said I went riding with Petra, or anyone else for that matter.'

'Harry...' Timothy growled.

'Okay, I went riding with Petra.'

'And? Crikey, man, I know guys don't talk about stuff like lurve and relationships, but this is me you're talking to.'

Harry chuckled, imagining his younger brother running a hand through his perpetually messy hair in exasperation. It was odd having the tables turned – in the past it had been Harry who had been trying to drag girlfriend details out of Timothy. His questioning had been more in the vein of "where the hell were you last night, and why didn't you tell me you wouldn't be home?"

'And...we kissed,' he admitted, a huge grin on his face.

'Yes!' Timothy shouted.

Harry jumped and held the phone away from his ear and Timothy's yell. 'Calm down, Tim, it was only a kiss.'

'For you, a kiss is a momentous occasion. When's the wedding? I feel an urge to buy one of those hats with the netting over your face and a feather in it.'

'You are **not** wearing a hat to my wedding.'

'Ah ha! So you are hoping it'll get serious?' Timothy teased.

'I'm hoping no such thing. I plan on taking it slowly and one step at a time and see where it goes.'

'Don't take it too slow,' his brother warned. 'She might lose interest and go find someone livelier.'

'Are you saying I'm boring?'

Timothy's voice sobered as he said, 'You are the least boring person I know.' Then the cockiness was back with a vengeance as he added, 'Except for me, of course. Seriously, if you like her, don't hang about. Life's too short and too damn unpredictable.'

Timothy was right. It was. And he should know.

'You've got a face like a slapped arse,' Amos pointed out when Petra popped in for a spot of lunch. 'What's wrong. Has lover-boy upset you? I saw you go out for a ride with him yesterday.'

'Don't call him that! And I haven't spoken to him today.'

Amos smirked knowingly. 'I see.'

'See what?'

'The reason for the glum face is because he hasn't phoned you.'

'I don't care if he hasn't phoned me,' she protested. But she was lying, she did care, even though she didn't expect him to be in touch so soon. But that wasn't the reason for her discontent. In fact, she wasn't sure why she was restless and disgruntled. She just **was**.

Yesterday had been wonderful (the kissing part especially) and her insides glowed with the memory of how he had hesitated at first, his lips tentative against hers, but then he'd crushed her to him and kissed her so deeply and thoroughly she'd thought she might faint. And when they'd broken apart, she'd found herself wobbly-legged and breathless, and longing for more.

He'd helped her mount Hercules, although she was perfectly capable of launching herself onto the horse's back by herself, and they'd ridden back in delighted silence.

She hadn't known what to say, and it seemed he hadn't either, but they shared several lingering looks and the occasional smouldering glance, and she had to be content with that. There had been too many people around when they'd clattered into the yard for him to kiss her again, although she'd desperately wanted him to. So they'd hidden their feelings and she'd said goodbye as though he was another customer that she'd taken out for a hack.

But that wasn't the reason for her mood today.

Something was wrong, she could sense it; she just didn't know what it was.

Heidi and May slid from their ponies' saddles with a little help from their respective parents. Petra listened to their excited chatter as Heidi told her mum, Rose Walker, all about her lesson. May was a little more subdued, and Petra put that down to her dad missing the thrilling sight of his young daughter attempting the first stage in her jumping career, which consisted of walking the pony over a pole lying on the ground. The pony in question was a rather good jumper, but he was also well-versed in having novice riders on his back, and he knew what was expected of him.

For six-year-old May, though, this was a brand-new and dangerous experience, and she'd expected her father to have witnessed it.

'Sorry I'm late, pumpkin, I got stuck in traffic,' he said, giving Petra a sheepish smile.

Petra smiled as May pushed home her unexpected advantage over her father. May was always brought to her lessons by her mum, who then had to shoot off, and her dad picked her up. Petra knew he tried not to miss a single minute of it, but sometimes he was late. Whenever he was, May insisted on being allowed to stroke the "big horses", instead of being taken straight home.

With an exaggerated sigh her father agreed, and Petra watched the little girl dart off in the direction of the stables, her dad following more sedately behind.

'See you next week,' he called over his shoulder and Petra nodded.

It was great to see the little ones come to her stables, many of them not having sat on the back of a horse before, and leaving at the end of their lessons full of wonder and delight at being able to control an animal so very much bigger than they were. Of course, it didn't happen all at once, but after a year of lessons May, in particular, was doing brilliantly.

Petra frowned as she checked the time. Harry still hadn't called. Maybe it was unreasonable to expect him to. She didn't have a great deal of experience when it came to dating, so she might be expecting too much from him. But there had been a definite connection between them – she didn't doubt that was true.

Having shortened the ponies' stirrups so they were resting on the saddle and not slapping against the animals' sides as she led them into their stalls for the night, Petra was surprised to see Charity hurrying towards her, a look of concern on her face.

'Charity? What's wrong?'

'I think you should come and see this. May Halligan dragged her dad off to pet the bigger horses, and when she came back I heard her ask her dad why Hercules was trying to kick himself in the tummy, and did he have an itch. I went to check on him and...' Charity paused and Petra felt her blood turn to ice. 'I think he might have colic.'

'Here, see to these,' she said, thrusting the reins into Charity's hands, and shouting 'Please,' as she shot to the door.

Not colic, please not colic, she prayed as she scurried out of the arena and down the row of stables. It was still quite light out, but she flicked the master switch on as she ran past, illuminating the yard and the individual stalls. She wanted to have a thorough look at the horse in good light, before she called the vet.

Petra heard Hercules before she saw him. He was pawing the concrete floor of his stable, which wasn't an unusual thing for a horse to do as they churned up the deep straw bedding under their feet, but she also heard a loud bang, signifying a steel-shod hoof had connected with the wooden partition of his stall.

When the bang was followed by a squeal, dread swept over her.

Those were the sounds of an animal in distress, and she was abruptly aware that this was what must have been bothering her all day. Animals were far, far better at hiding pain and discomfort than people were, and she must have subconsciously noticed that Hercules wasn't quite himself earlier. It was a damned pity that her conscious mind hadn't also noticed, because colic was the number one reason for horses having to be euthanised. The sooner it was treated the greater was the chance of his survival.

Steeling herself, she looked inside his stall.

The horse stood with his head hanging down, a sheen of sweat darkening the hair on his neck. His ears were laid back and his nostrils were flared.

When he uttered another squeal and brought one of his hind legs up to kick at his flank, Petra flinched.

It was colic, all right. The signs were unmistakable.

With a desperate look at the stricken animal, Petra ran to the house. 'Amos! Amos! Call the vet – Hercules has colic. Then can you phone Nathan to help me move him into the barn?'

Amos appeared from the kitchen, wiping his hands on the apron he liked to wear whilst he was cooking. He gave her a brief nod, his expression grave, and she heard his steps on the parquet floor of the hall as he hurried off to make the phone calls.

Petra hurried outside again, this time heading for the barn. There were a couple of chickens scratching about and Tiddles glared down at her from the top of several bales of hay where the cat had probably been waiting for mice to appear as dusk fell, but she couldn't see anything to hurt Hercules.

By the time she'd returned to the animal's stall, Amos was marching across the yard.

'The vet will be as quick as he can,' her uncle said. 'Have you been inside Hercules's stable yet?'

She shook her head. 'I wanted to wait for Nathan.' Hercules could be unpredictable sometimes; he was temperamental and highly-strung when he was upset, and although he wouldn't deliberately hurt her, she didn't want to take the risk of him lashing out because of the pain.

But neither could she leave him in his stall. Horses with colic had a tendency to roll onto their backs in an effort to relieve their painful stomachs, and if he rolled within the confines of his stable he might injure his legs on the walls of the stall as he thrashed around or, worse, he might not have enough room to get back up again. It was imperative she took him into the barn where she could also keep him moving. Walking a horse with colic could help to relieve the symptoms and the movement encouraged the gut to keep working, which in turn sometimes helped to relieve the pain.

Hercules lashed out with a hind leg, his hoof connecting with the wooden wall and a loud crash reverberated throughout the small space, making her wince.

'How long did Nathan say he'd be?' she asked – the sooner they got the horse out of his stable the better.

'I couldn't get hold of him. You'll have to make do with me.'

Petra bit her lip. 'Are you sure you'll be okay?' Amos never spoke of his angina, but that didn't stop her worrying about it and she knew he'd been advised not to overexert himself.

'I'll be fine,' he insisted, and all she could do was take her uncle's word for it.

She held out her hand, her arm inside the stall, and clicked her tongue. 'Come here, lad,' she crooned. 'Let me take a look at you, boy.'

The horse tossed his head, the whites of his eyes showing, but he stepped forward until he was close enough to the door for Petra to reach for his halter. Expertly she clipped a lead rope onto the metal ring underneath his chin.

Then she looked at her uncle, nodded, and opened the door.

Hercules lunged out, immediately crabbing sideways, but she hung on to the rope and the horse settled enough for Amos to get a second lead rope clipped onto his halter. With two of them controlling the animal, they should be able to get him into the barn.

'Are you okay?' she asked Amos again, her attention on the horse. She had to remain alert – a horse in pain might try to rear or bolt, kick or bite, but Hercules was relatively calm considering the circumstances.

'For the moment,' her uncle replied, and she knew it wouldn't be long before he started to struggle, and fresh worry gnawed at her.

He was already starting to look a little blue about the lips, but she didn't know whether that was from the chill of the spring evening air, or because he was feeling unwell.

Without wasting any more time, Petra led the horse towards the barn, Amos hanging onto the other lead rope, and between them they managed to get Hercules inside without incident.

As soon as the barn door was closed, Petra unclipped one of the lead ropes. 'I can take it from here,' she said to her uncle.

'I think I should stay.' He leant against one of the bales of hay and she could hear him wheezing. He didn't look at all well.

'How about if you go into the yard and wait for the vet?' she suggested. 'And take one of your heart pills before you do,' she added sternly. She knew what he could be like – he tended to deny he had a problem and sometimes she had to badger him not to do too much or nag him to take his medication.

Amos gave her a long look before nodding, and she sighed with relief. Her uncle had had enough excitement for one evening.

'You could bring me a sandwich later?' she suggested as she began walking Hercules around in a wide circle. She knew from experience that it was going to be a long night, and she also knew Amos liked to be useful. If all he could do was keep her fed and watered, then that would be enough.

All she could do was to keep the horse moving and try not to worry.

The first was easy – it was the latter she was having trouble with.

Harry was dozing in front of the tv and thinking he should take himself off to bed when his phone rang. He considered ignoring it – he'd had a long day and it was late – but it might be a customer. It wasn't unheard of for someone who wanted an animal to be shod to call him at an ungodly hour. Or it might be his brother, he thought suddenly, and a frisson of fear made the hairs on his arms stand on end.

Hoping nothing was wrong, he scrabbled around for his mobile.

'Petra?' He recognised the number immediately.

'It's Amos here, Petra's uncle.'

'Oh, hi.' Please don't tell me something has happened to her, Harry prayed, his mouth suddenly dry and his heart pounding. 'Is anything wrong?'

'It's Petra. She needs some help. I can't get hold of Nathan, and I'd do it myself but...'

'Do what? What help does she need?' Harry could hear the older man's harsh and fast breathing down the phone.

'One of the horses has colic.' Amos coughed and Harry waited for him to catch his breath. 'The vet came out a couple of hours ago. He thinks it's gas and maybe an impacted gut from Hercules chewing his stable door.'

Harry closed his eyes briefly. Hercules must have been feeling a little off-colour yesterday which would explain how Midnight had been able to keep up with him.

Amos carried on, 'He's been given a laxative to get things moving again, and a tranquiliser to help with the pain, and now Petra is walking him. She's going to be at it all night.'

As Amos was speaking, Harry was already changing out of his slouchy jogging bottoms and back into his work clothes. 'I'll be there in five minutes,' he said, grabbing his car keys.

Petra's uncle was waiting at the top of the lane for him, as Harry drove up. 'She's in the barn,' he said. 'I'll bring you a flask of coffee in a while.' He hesitated and seemed to be choosing his next words carefully. 'Thanks for coming. She might not show it, but she'll be pleased to see you.'

'It's what you do, when you care for someone,' Harry replied.

'I'm glad you feel that way, because I believe she cares for you, too.'

Embarrassed and delighted in equal measure, Harry said, 'I'll go on in, shall I?' He gestured towards the barn and the light leaking around the door.

Petra, Harry discovered, wasn't at all thrilled to see him. 'What are you doing here?' she demanded.

'I've come to help.'

'I don't need any.'

'I beg to differ.' It wasn't yet midnight and she was already looking exhausted. Hercules didn't look much better, and between them they'd worn a path through the compacted dirt which comprised the floor of the barn.

'You can beg all you like,' she retorted sharply. 'I'm fine doing this by myself.'

'Amos doesn't seem to think so.'

'Amos had no right to call you. I told him not to.'

'I'm glad he did.'

'I'm not,' she grumbled.

Harry might have felt deflated by her attitude if Amos hadn't had warned him. He guessed she was tired and worried, and her original prickliness had reasserted itself as a coping and defence mechanism. She was so used to managing on her own that he thought maybe she'd forgotten how to accept help from anyone, no matter whether she cared about them or not. And no matter whether they cared about her.

As Harry walked over to her and took the lead rope out of her hand, ignoring her protests, he came to the conclusion that he more than cared for her. He was falling in love with her. She might have more thorns than a holly bush, she might be proud, stubborn and independent to the point of causing him despair, but he didn't care. It was what made her, her. And he loved her for it.

He also loved her for her caring nature, for her love of her horses, for the odd moments when she let her guard down and allowed the sun to shine out of her.

He loved her for her dedication, for her passion and for her strength. He also loved her for her vulnerability.

And this was where he stepped in.

She no longer had to cope alone. If she'd let him, he'd give her as much support as she needed and probably more than she wanted.

If she'd let him...

'I'm here now, let me take a turn at walking him,' he said, leading the horse on yet another circuit of the barn. He watched her go to the nearest pile of bales and sink down onto one of them, then he turned his attention to Hercules.

The horse didn't look good. But he didn't look as bad as Harry had feared, either. Sweat had dried on his neck and flanks, leaving a white tide of salt on his coat. He was walking willingly and not kicking up a fuss, but the droop of his head and the plod of his hooves told Harry that Hercules had had enough. The poor guy was tired, and although Harry would love nothing better than to let the horse rest, he knew it was better to keep him moving.

And throughout that long night, that was what the two of them did, taking it in turns to walk Hercules around and around the barn, with Amos popping in frequently to check on progress and bringing them fresh coffee and snacks to keep them going. During one of Petra's turns, Harry rearranged a couple of bales of hay to form a makeshift couch, and he found some horse rugs which had been neatly folded away until next winter when the horses and ponies would need them again. He spread two of them across the couch and used another to drape over himself. It grew chilly if you didn't keep moving and even the gentle pace of the circuits they were doing helped to keep the blood flowing, but the one who was sitting out was at risk of frostbite.

Queenie, bless her, did her best to keep the both of them warm, curling up next to whichever one of them was sitting it out but despite the furry hot water bottle, the dipping temperature, the worry and the tiredness gradually began to take its toll.

Petra looked shattered and Harry guessed he probably didn't look much better.

Then, finally, as the witching hour clicked over to four a.m. Hercules farted.

It was an incredibly long and drawn out affair, and after an initial gasp of relief,

Petra started to laugh. Harry chuckled too.

The horse broke wind again, louder and longer than the last time, then they were laughing so hard tears streamed down their cheeks and Harry doubled over with the force of it.

The horse's ears pricked and his dark, liquid eyes gazed from one to the other. Even Queenie wondered what was going on, and she whined uncertainly until Harry tickled her under the chin.

'I think we can safely say Hercules is over the worst of it,' Harry said.

It was what they had been waiting for. The horse wasn't out of the woods yet, but the release of so much trapped gas meant movement was afoot. The next milestone would be the appearance of poop.

They didn't have long to wait.

During the following half an hour, Hercules seemed to take great delight in dropping little presents all over the floor of the barn. He looked perkier too, more like his old self.

'Let me,' Petra said, getting to her feet and coming over to him.

'You've got ten minutes before it's your turn. Make the most of it,' Harry joked.

'It's my horse, my rules, and I want a go.'

She was smiling as she said it, the first smile Harry had seen since he'd arrived, so he handed her the lead rope and sat down next to Queenie, who huffed out a deep sigh at being disturbed yet again by these pesky humans. She edged over to him and rested her head on his lap, then shut her eyes tightly, intent on trying to get back to sleep.

Harry poured himself another cup of coffee from the flask. It wasn't as hot as he liked it, so he set it to one side, had a drink of water instead, and watched Petra stroke Hercules. Her nose was close to the horse's and he could hear her murmuring to the animal, soothing and reassuring him.

Harry closed his eyes for a moment.

'Queenie likes you,' Petra said, jerking him awake and he cleared his throat, hoping she hadn't noticed he'd been dozing. 'She doesn't normally bother with anyone other than me and Amos.'

'I like her, too. She's a sweetie.'

She was also warm snuggled against him and soft, and he absent-mindedly stroked her silky ears as he watched the spaniel's mistress resume her trudge around the barn.

Harry knew Petra would keep this up until the vet returned in the morning to check on Hercules, and once again silence descended, the relief of knowing the horse was getting better superseded by exhaustion.

When he took his turn for the umpteenth time that night, Harry was conscious of just how quiet it was. There were no sounds apart from the muffled thud of the horse's hooves, the creak of the barn's beams contracting as the chill of the night deepened, and the rustle as something moved in the straw.

It was surreal, as though they were on another planet, or in another era. Nothing outside the barn existed. The world had shrunk to the two of them, the horse and the dog.

The next time he walked close to the hay-couch, Harry's gaze came to rest on Petra and he smiled softly; she was fast asleep, her eyelids fluttering, her fingers twitching. Queenie was awake, guarding her mistress, but her tail thumped with approval as Harry broke off his horse-walking to drape another rug over Petra and tuck it in around her. Then he took his jacket off, pulled his fleece over his head, folded it into a pillow and eased it under her head.

Petra shifted slightly and made a cute little noise, but she didn't wake, which

Harry was pleased about. She needed the rest and he could handle things from here.

As he put his jacket back on and zipped it up, his eyes roamed over her face, thinking how vulnerable she looked in sleep, and how beautiful. It had hurt him to see her so upset, and as he stood there he made a silent vow to himself and to her – he intended to do anything and everything in his power not to let her feel that way again. He had an overwhelming urge to protect her, to look after her, to cherish her. To love her.

If only she would let him...

Petra screwed her eyes shut as tight as they would go. She didn't want to wake up. She was stiff, cold and uncomfortable, but it was too much of an effort to re-join the world of the sentient.

Then the memory of last night flashed into her head and she sat up with a start.

It was early; the sun had only just risen, she guessed from the light creeping around the edge of the barn door. The dawn chorus was in full flow outside, but it was strangely quiet inside.

Harry, she saw, was slumped in a corner of the hay-couch and when his eyes met hers, he smiled, and she knew everything was all right. Hercules was dozing in the way horses do, with his head down and one hind foot cocked, the hoof's tip resting on the ground. A huge pile of poo had built up on the floor behind him, and never had Petra been so pleased to see so much manure. He was going to be fine; he was fine.

She got to her feet to check, nevertheless.

As soon as she was satisfied that her initial assessment was correct, her attention came back to Harry. He was fine too; he had dark shadows under his eyes, his shoulders were slumped and stubble coated his chin, but he'd be as right as rain after a nice long sleep.

It hadn't escaped her notice that at some point when she'd been sleeping, he'd slipped his fleece under her head and thrown another rug over her. It gave her a warm glow to think he'd cared enough to do such a thing.

'He's doing okay,' he said, getting awkwardly to his feet.

'So I see. I'm sorry I fell asleep.'

'Don't be. Hercules and I were fine on our own.'

She smiled. 'So I see,' she repeated.

Petra moved closer to him, reached out a hand and slipped it into his, lacing her fingers through his.

Harry gently squeezed her hand.

She leant into him, her head resting on his shoulder. He kissed her hair.

Then he kissed her forehead.

She lifted her face to his. 'Thank you.'

'There's nothing to thank me for.'

'I think there is. Not everyone would stay up all night to help a friend.'

'Is that all I am – a friend?' She heard the dismay in his voice.

'Yes, you are. But you're also more than that.'

'I am?' He sounded a little more hopeful

She nodded, enjoying teasing him if only for a moment; she knew how she felt about him. And she knew Amos was right. She wasn't going to leave it too late – she didn't intend to let this wonderful man slip through her fingers. He was kind, considerate, thoughtful, fun to be with, and he loved horses as much as she did. What more could she ask for?

Actually, there **was** one thing...

'You are...I mean...'

She was lost for words. She knew what she wanted to say but she didn't know how to say it. She didn't know if she should. Panic and fear held her back. If he didn't feel the same way about her, she'd be devastated.

Harry came to her rescue yet again. He cupped her face in his hands, his lips inches from hers. 'I love you,' he said.

'Yes, that's it,' she whispered. 'That's exactly what I wanted to say.'

And it was also the other thing she asked for; that he loved her.

From the look in his eyes, she realised that he did.

Finally, for Petra, as for everything else on Muddypuddle Lane, spring had brought new love, new hope, and a brand new beginning.

The Stables on Muddypuddle Lane Series

Spring

Summer

Autumn

Winter

Valentine Kisses

The Patter of Tiny Feet

Wedding Bells

Christmas

About Etti

Etti Summers is the author of wonderfully romantic fiction with happy ever afters guaranteed.

She is also a wife, a mum, a pink gin enthusiast, a veggie grower and a keen reader.